FOREVER
SUMMER

ALSO BY JENNY OLIVER

Chelsea High

FOREVER SUMMER

JENNY OLIVER

ELECTRIC MONKEY

First published in Great Britain 2021 by Electric Monkey, part of Farshore
An imprint of HarperCollins*Publishers*
1 London Bridge Street, London SE1 9GF

farshore.co.uk

HarperCollins*Publishers*
1st Floor, Watermarque Building, Ringsend Road, Dublin 4, Ireland

ISBN 978 1 4052 9506 2

Printed and bound in Great Britain by CPI Group

1

Typeset by Avon DataSet Ltd, Alcester, Warwickshire

For Ruth, for all the adventures.

CHAPTER ONE

My future self would be jealous of this moment.

I was lying on the soft grass of Central Park, New York City, my head resting on the sun-warmed T-shirt of my boyfriend, Ezra Montgomery, as we sipped iced coffee and watched baseball players practising their pitches.

It still sent a rush through me to say my boyfriend, Ezra.

Whenever I looked at him, it made me realise that through all the chaos and the bad stuff, sometimes things go exactly right. Exactly how you want them to.

Yesterday we went up the Empire State, he laughed at how amazed I was, we cycled over to Brooklyn and rummaged through vintage shops. Last night was a film premiere. Afterwards we walked the streets of Soho in the dark, eating ice cream, and fell asleep on the giant cream sofas of his family's Manhattan penthouse. This morning, we wolfed down stacks of pancakes with maple syrup and fresh juice in a diner with low lights and turquoise booth seats.

All this he'd done a million times before. For me it was a novelty. I'd never even been on a plane before.

As Ezra and I lay in the haze of sunshine, I wished the

moment could be paused in time. Because right there, right then, I was living the fairy tale.

'Don't go home,' Ezra said, arms tightening around me.

I laughed. 'OK, I won't.'

I could feel him smile.

In the distance I could hear the crack of a baseball on a bat in the nets. Traffic. The yapping of dogs. Above us perfect white fluffy clouds blocked out the glare of the sun.

'It's rubbish here on my own,' Ezra said, lying back, propped up on his elbows.

'You're not on your own. You have your tutor,' I joked. I'd met the very stern private tutor his parents had hired so he kept up to date with the UK curriculum.

'Great!' Ezra rolled his eyes.

'It's not for much longer,' I said. 'You'll be back by the autumn.'

Ezra said, 'Yeah,' as if trying to convince himself.

When Ezra had offered to pay for my ticket to New York, I'd immediately declined. No matter the fact it was small change to him, I couldn't accept something that expensive. But then his tone had changed and he'd said, 'How about if I said I was asking as a favour for me? I need you here, Norah. Just to keep me sane.'

Well, how could I say no? Even my mum was on board. 'You deserve something lovely,' she'd said, and smiled.

In Central Park, the clouds slid away and the sun dazzled.

The grass tickled. I twisted in Ezra's arms so we were face to face. So close I could see flecks of violet in his brown eyes. 'It'll be OK.'

Ezra's family were in New York for pioneering treatment for his brother, Josh, who had almost fallen to his death on holiday in Cornwall. The fact he'd been secretly following his heroic big brother up a crumbling cliff at the time was something Ezra was still struggling to come to terms with.

Ezra sighed, resting his forehead against mine. 'I'm so pleased you're here.'

I smiled. 'Me too.'

I moved so I could lie next to him, head on his shoulder. I could smell the fresh cut grass and the familiar warmth and washing-powder scent of him. I shut my eyes, just to inhale, already nostalgic for that moment. Then I moved so my palms were flat on his chest, my chin resting on the backs of my hands, and looked at the bow of his lips, the point of his nose, and the clean, sharp line of his cheekbones.

He still had his eyes shut. 'Are you looking up my nose?' he asked.

I laughed.

He suddenly grabbed me tight and rolled over so he was on top of me. 'I'll really miss you, Norah Whittaker,' he said.

And I said, 'I'll miss you, Ezra Montgomery.'

Then he kissed me, long and slow, the sunlight dancing on my closed eyelids.

When I opened my eyes he was looking down at me.

'I think I love you.'

The word love hung in the air. Neither of us had ever said it before. I felt my heart skip.

'You think or you know?' I asked.

'I know.'

Ezra looked suddenly bashful, maybe embarrassed. I bit my lip to stop the beaming smile I felt beneath the surface. Then his expression changed, suddenly all hooded eyes and serious as he said, 'I definitely love you.'

'I love you too,' I said.

And he said, 'You don't have to say it just because I did,' pushing his too-long hair back from his eyes.

'I know.'

His lips tilted into a half-smile. 'OK then,' he said. 'Good.'

A few days later, it was all just as I had predicted. Cycling to school through the bleak grey London drizzle for the start of the summer term at Chelsea High, the jealousy I felt for my former self was almost painful.

I was so tired as I pulled up to the curb. I'd flown back on the red-eye and spent yesterday in and out of a jetlagged haze. But my memories of Ezra were more than enough to make it all bearable.

Everyone arriving at school was fresh from Easters spent skiing in Klosters and Megève or, for the chosen few, Coco

Summers' St Moritz chalet. They hugged and air-kissed on the steps, comparing their snow tans while snapping selfies and stalking into school as chauffeurs pulled away.

It was so different from my old school. Back then, we never left the little Thames-side Mulberry Island because everything we wanted was on our doorstep – the river to swim in, the meadow to laze in, our friends and a dilapidated basketball court. Now I was at Chelsea High and I too was fresh off the plane from an exotic holiday. I looked up at the giant red-brick building with its turrets, flags and stained glass. Was I one of them now?

A dark green Range Rover pulled up beside me, straight through a puddle, drenching my legs. Great.

A blond guy got out of the back seat. Didn't even notice me. The car was already pulling back out into the traffic.

'Hey!' I called.

The blond guy turned. 'What?'

'You just soaked me.'

'Well, don't stand next to a puddle,' he said, like the fault could only be mine. He laughed, all mocking green gaze, then took the steps two at a time up to the doors of the school.

No, I wasn't one of them. I reluctantly followed him up the steps, past the gold plaque gleaming with the Chelsea High motto, *Vincere fecit* – made to win. I would never be one of them.

I had my own motto now to get me through till the end of the year. *Ezra loves me*. And already I was smiling.

CHAPTER TWO

I still had trouble believing that my bohemian parents had once been part of this rich elite. After my dad was arrested for fraud, my surprisingly rich grandparents had paid for the lawyers and arranged a flash new mooring for us in Battersea, where our scruffy old houseboat stuck out like a sore thumb and the neighbours whispered about us disapprovingly. My grandparents paid my school fees now.

We could never go back to Mulberry Island, or the life we'd had before. My dad had lost too much of our friends' money. Now me and my mum were living a life on pause while he served his jail sentence. We struggled to find our place in a world where we no longer fitted.

I filed down the dark corridors of Chelsea High into assembly, breathing in the smell of cleaning products and old money. Coco Summers and her gang sashayed ahead of me. Most people knew Coco from Instagram. I knew her because she was Ezra's ex-girlfriend. If it was up to Coco, they'd still be together. I was now the constant target of her furious jealousy. Deep down, I was sure there was an insecure little girl inside Coco, but she kept her well hidden.

The main buzz seemed to be about Coco's new hair. All the kids in the year below were nudging each other to look. Gone was her giant white-blonde cloud, and in its place were tousled beach waves in tumbling shades of caramel.

'It's what Vox wanted,' Coco was telling her gang, running her hands through the glossy curls.

I'd probably have known what she was talking about if I hadn't muted her on Instagram at the beginning of the holidays. I couldn't stomach the multiple shots of her picture-perfect ski chalet, or Coco and her pure evil BFF, Verity Benitez, in matching fur hats and all-in-one Gucci ski suits posing under a giant stag's head.

'Vox?' I whispered to my friend Daniel as we trooped into the Great Hall. 'As in the fashion brand?'

'Keep up, Norah,' he said as we sat down. 'She's the new face of the brand.'

I do Art and Drama with Daniel. He's one of the few funny, normal people at Chelsea High.

In front of us, Coco was saying, 'They're just launching the new Midsummer perfume. Apparently they had me in mind when they blended the scent.'

A voice from the row behind cut in. 'I dread to think what it smells like then.'

Coco's eyes narrowed. The boys in her gang smirked – the tall, loping redhead, Rollo Cooper-Quinn, and Freddie Chang with his wide, elastic grin and jet-black hair tied back in a little knot.

I turned, wondering who had the nerve to so casually attack Coco Summers. It was the same blond guy who'd sauntered out of the Range Rover that morning. Broad shoulders, dark eyebrows and a freckled ski tan. His high cheekbones and eyes that narrowed wickedly as they smiled made him seem strangely familiar.

With a casual shake of her mane, Coco said silkily, 'When I want your opinion, brother dearest, I'll ask for it.'

Her brother?

He smiled. Equally silky. Now I could see the resemblance. They had the same presence. They both emanated entitlement. The world owed them a favour because they had deigned to live in it.

The headmaster strode on to the stage. 'Good morning, students.' His teeth were whiter than ever. 'I am delighted to welcome you back for what I hope will be a fantastic summer at Chelsea High.'

'I didn't know Coco had a brother,' I whispered to Daniel, who was trying to have a snooze with his chin in his hand.

'How can you not know about Laurent Summers?' Daniel thought about this, yawning. 'Actually, I suppose he's been in Argentina for a while. And you *are* always the last to know everything.'

'Laurent?' I repeated the name, intrigued. 'What was he doing in Argentina?'

Daniel made a face like he didn't really care. 'Training with a polo guru or something. I don't know. Probably just having a good time, knowing Laurent.'

I snuck another look at Coco's brother. He was lounging back, surveying the place with an air of cocky self-assurance.

'And the school didn't mind?' I said.

The headmaster was droning on in the background.

Daniel raised an eyebrow. 'Norah, have you learned nothing about the Summers family? Money talks.'

That should be the motto for the school, I thought, looking at all the perfect, polished faces around me. Entitled and effortlessly pleased with themselves. They lived by a different set of rules here. It was no wonder I was always one step behind.

From her chair at the end of the row, Mrs Pearce, our form tutor, leaned over. 'Norah, Daniel, shush!'

'Gladly.' Daniel closed his eyes again.

The headmaster read out some mundane notices. Then he clapped his hands, his face alight. 'And now for the most important announcement –'

In front of me, I heard Verity murmur quietly to Coco, 'Emmeline Chang has found love in the big, strong, muscular arms of Rollo Cooper-Quinn.'

My head jerked up.

'I'm proud to announce that the annual Inter-School Sports Tournament will be held this year at our very own Chelsea High,' the headmaster went on. 'This is a great privilege for the school, and something to make sure that your parents and any alumni have in their calendars. On home ground we really do expect wins from you all. So get training. No excuses.' He surveyed the sea of faces. 'It is exceptionally good timing to have back in the fold our very own champion, Laurent Summers, who will no doubt captain the Chelsea High polo team to a magnificent victory.'

Laurent didn't even blush as the headmaster led a round of applause.

I was too busy looking for Emmeline to join in. To my horror, she really was sitting snuggled next to Rollo, with his big arm draped possessively across her thigh.

Emmeline Chang – French Korean, impossibly beautiful with waist-length hair and an addiction to reading – was one of my other main friends here. Her and Daniel made the place bearable. If she was going out with Rollo, then she would be sucked into Coco's orbit and I'd never see her.

I watched Rollo twine his fingers through Emmeline's. She caught me looking, and her face coloured with a self-conscious blush, proud but embarrassed. I gave her a surprised thumbs-up because she looked so sweetly awkward.

'*Rollo*?' I whispered to Daniel. 'But Emmeline's so clever!'

'And he's so stupid?' Daniel replied. 'Opposites really do attract.'

'Norah! Daniel!' Mrs Pearce chastised again.

'And of course, the Sports Tournament will be rounded

off with the annual Variety Performance, which I expect to be a celebration of our victories,' continued the headmaster. 'Audition dates will be circulated by your form tutors.'

Beside me Daniel perked up. He was co-running the Variety Show with head of Drama, Mr Benson. 'You're doing it, yeah?' he said to me.

I shook my head. 'No.'

That finally woke him up. 'What do you mean, *no*? Norah, you'd be one of the leads.'

'I'm playing netball.'

'Who cares about netball?' he asked in distaste.

I shrugged, non-committal. It was a poor excuse and he knew it, but I wasn't up to explaining how my voice stuck in my throat like tar every time I thought about singing now. My lifelong ambition to be an actress was too tied up with memories of my dad.

Me and him were at our happiest on stage. Singing and acting was synonymous with life. It was what we lived and breathed. My dad had always been on the cusp of hitting the big time, but never quite got the break. I grew up listening to his stories of auditions, the smell of stage make-up, the heat of the lights. It was all I'd ever wanted to do and be.

But now he was in jail, a shadow of his former larger-than-life self.

My dad had always wanted to do everything quick. He had an infectious energy for life and never wanted to wait.

So when a scheme came along that promised to make him rich *and* a star – one that funded feature films – he didn't ask questions. He just jumped. He wasn't the kind of person who read the small print. Of course, it was a scam. Soon he was in too deep to get out. And now he was paying for his mistakes.

To sing now felt like a betrayal. Made my chest tighten at the memory of our happiness. I had to find a new dream for the future.

'Norah, you *have* to audition!' Daniel urged.

Mrs Pearce saved me from having to answer by clicking her fingers and saying, 'Daniel, get over here, now!' and pointing to the space next to her chair.

'This isn't finished,' Daniel told me, getting up.

The headmaster was still talking. 'If you're not in a sport, do audition. We expect to see all our pupils giving back to the school in one form or another. And on that note, to finish off today's assembly, I'd like to welcome to the stage Coco Summers, who has some thrilling news to share with the school. Coco?'

'Oh, that's me.' Coco giggled, like she'd forgotten. She skipped up to the front, hair billowing, and hopped on the stage.

'So!' she said, all gesticulating arms and shimmering pink lips. 'That's great about the Tournament and the Variety Performance. Go, Chelsea High!' She did a whoop and everyone laughed. 'But before all that, I have some *incredible* news that could involve some of you guys.'

An excited ripple ran through the crowd. I watched Mr Watts, my Maths teacher, fold his arms and purse his lips with disapproving interest.

Coco went on. 'As you know, I have been chosen as the face of the new Midsummer perfume for the brand Vox.' She paused to allow applause, seeming to grow as she spoke, fuelled by the adoration. 'And they want to shoot a commercial on a gorgeous Greek Island featuring a group of us from Chelsea High!' Another pause. More gasps and claps. 'So the one and only Margot de Souza, head of Vox, will be coming here, to pick out who will star alongside me!'

Cue squeals of wild excitement.

God I missed Ezra. A wry eye-roll would have had us both suppressing laughter. Instead, I was surrounded by frenetic whispers and giddy preening.

From the row behind, I heard Laurent Summers' cut-glass voice drawl, 'God help us all.'

CHAPTER THREE

I came home to an empty boat. Since my dad was in jail and my mum had gone back to full-time work, I always came home to an empty boat.

Mum's new job was at Hudson and Sons, a company that supplied the shirts old men bought from places like Marks and Spencer, or that were advertised in the back of bird-watching magazines. It wasn't the worst job, but it sounded pretty dry when she bitched about it. Her job as designer seemed to involve choosing between white plastic buttons or mother-of-pearl.

'Men,' her boss, Frank Hudson Junior, had told her in the interview, 'do not like change.'

I wondered if anyone liked change.

We were a world away now from Mum's old vintage clothes stall at Portobello market, where tourists bought Hawaiian shirts and eccentric regulars picked old nylon shell suits and big feathered hats. Even wrapped up against the frost at five in the morning to set up the stall, I had loved it. But what I missed the most was my mum's smile when she picked out the perfect vintage gown for an indecisive customer, or shook her head at the terrible jokes cracked by Big Dave at the army surplus stall. It was ages since I'd heard her laugh.

I dumped my bag and went to look in the fridge for something to eat. The summer rain tapped gently on the glass, flattening the river water and spattering off the ducks sheltering on our deck.

There was very little food in. I had a bowl of Weetabix and sat at the little kitchen counter, kicking my leg against the cupboard, wondering if anyone had taken our Portobello pitch yet, or if there was just an outline on the floor like at a murder scene. *Here lies the remains of the best second-hand clothes stall in London and the smiles of everyone who worked there.*

I thought of my mum's best friend and old business partner, Jackie. We hardly saw her any more. Jackie claimed she was too old to run the stall on her own. What would she think of us now? Our world had shrunk, with us just waiting out the years till my dad came home. Counting them down on a giant invisible calendar. Trying our best to live a normal life in between prison visits. Psyching ourselves up every month for the sadness of seeing him.

I couldn't think about it too much. That first visit when I'd felt the hands pat me down. Sat in my socks while they checked my shoes. And the smell . . . It got in your eyes, down your throat, lingered on your clothes and skin. I remember my dad shrugging and saying, 'It's fine. I hardly smell it any more.' And then, by the end of the visit, crumbling before our eyes,

16

sobbing into his hands. 'It's so awful. I can't bear it. It's killing me in here.'

I had tried so hard not to cry when I saw him, all grey-faced and greasy-haired. But when he cracked, I cracked. I knew what he'd done was wrong, but I wanted there to be a different punishment. I wanted to plead with the judge – *can't you see he's a good person? He's my dad!*

I was sick in the car park afterwards.

After that, it was as if we made a silent pact to pretend it had never happened. We all got through it our own way. My dad plastered a fake smile on his face. My mum started her new job. And I spent the hours when New York was awake on the phone to Ezra.

Finishing my Weetabix, I headed into my bedroom, which was little more than a box with a huge window at one end, just big enough for my bed. All my clothes were folded in drawers under the mattress. My dad built it so it was a bit wonky, and one of the drawers had never shut properly, but it was my favourite place in the world.

I had an hour to kill before Ezra was done with his tutor. I pulled on his old hockey hooded sweatshirt and lay staring out at the river, thinking of everything I could tell him about the first day of term. Trouble was, I'd spent most of it daydreaming about being back in New York with him. I had homework to do, but I didn't do it. Instead I closed my eyes and relived the trip for the ten millionth time.

CHAPTER FOUR

Coco was top of the pecking order for a reason. Bad stuff slid off her shiny surface. She was charismatic and funny and she made life exciting. She was like an addiction.

Our little group of Daniel, Emmeline and me quietly disbanded. Emmeline's relationship with Rollo pulled her towards Coco and her gang. Daniel, when he wasn't working on the Variety Performance, drifted after her.

Coco was loving all the attention. During English she whispered, 'Emmeline, Rollo, you're going to audition for my Vox advert, aren't you? I'm going to get us all there together. Margot de Souza has final say, of course, but I have influence.'

'Less talking, more listening, Coco,' Mrs Pearce called from up at the front. 'So, what did everyone read during the holidays? Emmeline, shall we start with you?'

Emmeline's cheeks coloured and she swallowed. 'Nothing actually,' she said, to Mrs Pearce's surprise. Emmeline was renowned for always being hidden behind a huge paperback classic.

'Who needs books when she's got me?' Rollo quipped.

Mrs Pearce looked very disparaging. I couldn't believe

my whip-smart friend had disappeared into her relationship so easily.

Lunch hours were the worst. I tried to hang out with Daniel, but that meant sitting on the periphery of Coco's gang, silent in her presence. And to make matters worse, my other friend, Tabitha, was on a Paris exchange this term as part of her music scholarship.

To my surprise, it was the impending Sports Tournament that gave me a viable alternative. The expectation from the headmaster for wins all round meant practises had been ratcheted up.

Sport was everything at Chelsea High. There was no opting out. I'd picked netball because I'd been good at it at Mulberry Island Academy. To my surprise, the netball coach, Ms Stowe, had thought I showed enough promise to be reserve for the team. I quite liked the training. It took my mind off everything going on at home, and gave me something tangible to focus on. I sat on the bench at matches, playing the occasional quarter, which suited me fine, unless it rained.

Unfortunately, I hadn't stuck to the holiday training schedule, so the laps of the sports field Ms Stowe had us doing were killing me.

'Problem, Norah?' Ms Stowe bellowed from the gate of the courts, stopwatch in hand. She was an ex-England goal attack, and her aspirations for glory meant she pushed her players to the limits.

I looked up, gasping, wishing I'd done a bit more jogging over the holidays. 'No, Miss!'

'Well, get on with it!'

The other reserve on the team was a girl called Malaika, who was in the year above me. She attempted a sympathetic smile.

Ms Stowe was having none of it. 'Focus, Malaika! There's too much slacking, we'll do another lap.'

I looked up in horror. I was knackered. My heart was beating so loud and hard, I wondered if I might pass out.

Malaika grimaced. She was as sweaty as me, skin glistening. Malaika's parents both worked for the foreign office. She'd grown up in Turkey, Italy and Greece, and had moved to the UK the previous year. She was fluent in five languages, though she spoke English with a slight American accent from all the international schools she'd attended. She was going out with a guy from a boarding school in Hampshire, and was also a killer netball shot, which meant she had more chance of getting off the reserve bench than me because I tended to lose my shooting skills under pressure.

At the mention of another set of laps, the team captain, Bettina, a six-foot blonde Dane, glared at me. 'Thanks a lot!' she spat, speeding past with vice-captain, Layla Bryant.

I pushed my damp hair from my face. 'It wasn't just me!' I protested, but, like the machine that she was, Bettina was already back in the zone.

The Vox auditions for Coco Summers' perfume advert

were taking place by the school hall. Everyone had suddenly had a new haircut and beautiful new highlights. Coco was strutting about the place, whispering promises of parts and giggling good lucks. The sky was bright blue and the sunshine bright, like even the weather wanted in.

'It's like the whole school's auditioning,' said Malaika as she and I jogged side by side, taking in the queue outside the hall.

They'd had to stagger the audition times. The queue snaked outside and round the corner, everyone sipping water or fiddling with their hair and make-up. The boys were trying to look nonchalant and cool, like they weren't interested but they were there all the same. Everyone had a number pinned to their front like it was The X Factor.

'You auditioning?' Malaika asked.

I shook my head. I couldn't imagine anything worse than a trip with Coco and co. Or the idea of all the people on Mulberry Island seeing me in a swanky perfume advert when my dad's double-dealings had left them all penniless and ruined. But there was something intoxicating about the anticipation of the waiting auditionees, their birdlike chatter and giddy grins, and I felt a tiny bit jealous.

'What about you?' I asked as Ms Stowe blew her whistle for us to hurry up.

Malaika was definitely beautiful enough to audition. She had immaculate bone structure and giant, almond-shaped eyes. 'No,' she said. 'I don't have the time allocation.'

'What do you mean?'

'I allocate my time according to my key major interests,' she said as we jogged on. 'I want to be a neuroscientist, so I do Science club with Mr Scott-Davidson. He's one of the best psychology professors there is. My dad says, you find the best and learn from them.' She wiped the sweat off her forehead. 'And I want to be on the netball team. Ms Stowe's one of the best in the country, so she works us hard. I also want to see my boyfriend. Like I said, I don't have the time allocation for modelling.'

As we passed the queue, she grinned. 'It would've been fun, though, wouldn't it? Island paradise, hair and make-up, on TV.'

No one here mentioned the hefty fee that came with the job. They didn't need to. They all had enough. I'd only seen it when I scanned the flyer pinned on the noticeboard. For me, money was the one factor that might have swayed it. It would be such a help to my mum that I felt a flicker of guilt for not even giving it a try.

'Don't know what you two are wittering on about,' said Bettina ahead of us. 'You wouldn't have been picked anyway!'

'Get on with it!' shouted Ms Stowe from the netball courts, hands on hips.

Next to us, on the field, some of the polo boys were warming down on ponies that were damp with sweat. Freddie Chang,

Ned Fitzgibbon, Emir Faez – whose media magnate father owned his own polo team in Abu Dhabi – Yannis Costopoulos and, of course, Coco's brother, Laurent Summers. The boys had mud and grass stains on their white trousers. Freddie had unbuckled his helmet and was wiping his damp hair with his hand. They all stopped to watch, astride their priceless ponies, as we jogged to the courts in our maroon netball skirts.

'Ladies,' Laurent said, bowing his head like a gentleman, though there was nothing gentlemanly in his expression.

Bettina beamed and blew him a kiss. Layla giggled.

'Don't stop, girls!' Ms Stowe hollered.

Laurent shouted back, 'Huge apologies, Ms Stowe. Didn't mean to distract.'

'Shut up, Summers!' Ms Stowe shouted, but her demeanour had cracked when subjected to the full force of Laurent's grin.

He blew her a kiss. Still laughing, he caught sight of me jogging at the back and said, 'Christ, don't kill yourself.'

I immediately flushed beetroot with humiliation.

Out of nowhere, the wind started to whip up around us. I heard a noise like thunder. Looking across, I saw a big black helicopter landing on the east rugby pitch. Clouds of dust rose from the ground and leaves were torn from the chestnut trees. The noise startled the ponies.

'What the hell!' Laurent looked furious, trying to calm his ride.

Freddie's palomino went nuts, eyes wild, ready to bolt.

As the helicopter noise increased and dust filled the air, Freddie's pony suddenly took off at a canter. Taken off guard, Freddie's helmet flew out of his hands. So did the reins. The pony was completely out of control and it looked like Freddie was about to fall hard – until Laurent cantered over. He grabbed the reins and pulled the terrified palomino up. Sliding off his own pony and getting right down close, he muttered some horse whisperer stuff to get the skittish beast to calm down.

The helicopter finally settled and the blades slowed. Laurent didn't take his eyes off the ponies, just whispering and stroking until the noise had completely stopped. Then he gave them both one last stroke on the nose and let Freddie's reins drop.

'Bloody hell, Laurent,' said Yannis, trotting up to where a shaky Freddie was climbing down from his pony. 'Where'd you learn to do that?'

'Do what?' Laurent asked, face jokey again.

'That!' said Freddie, now he'd got his voice back.

'It was amazing,' cooed Bettina with a flick of her long blonde hair.

Laurent jumped back on his horse, turning it in the direction of the clubhouse. 'Just something I picked up in Argentina,' he said smugly.

I turned away, annoyed at how impressed I had been.

CHAPTER FIVE

The helicopter pilot was opening the door for the passengers to disembark while the headmaster strode over to greet them. Coco pranced along behind him.

First out was a slim black guy with peroxide-blond hair. Dressed in a three-piece army-print suit and giant horn-rimmed glasses, he squinted against the afternoon sun as he jumped down from the chopper.

Behind him came Dame Margot de Souza, infamously eccentric aristocrat and owner of leading fashion house, Vox, a brand as famous for her as it was for its clothing. She struggled a little with the tiny cabin door because her dress was so huge. Her assistant went to help as she tottered about on platform trainers. In the crook of her arm was a bag shaped like a plastic doll, and she had a stuffed blackbird on her pillbox hat. She was magnificent. The sight of her was almost enough to make me want to audition, just to get a closer look. My mum would have been in heaven.

Coco squealed. 'It's so exciting you're here!'

Margot de Souza swept Coco up into a tulle-filled hug My opinion of the fashion grand-dame plummeted.

Ms Stowe's whistle trilled. 'Get a move on!'

It started to drizzle almost as soon as we began to play a game. The netball court and the ball got gradually wetter. I was in defence, marking Boo Clemency-Hall. Because of the rain, the ball kept slipping from my hands.

Bettina was spitting because we were losing. 'Get your act together, Norah.'

No one had been particularly good, especially Malaika.

'Malaika,' Ms Stowe raged as we drank water and wiped the rain off. She clicked her fingers in front of Malaika's face. 'Are you even with us?'

'She wants to be auditioning for the Vox advert, Miss,' said Layla slyly.

'I do not!' Malaika snapped, too quick.

'They all want to be there,' Layla added, as if she wasn't just as keen as the rest.

Ms Stowe was aghast. 'You want to do this too, Layla?'

'Not with her wonky face,' Bettina joked.

Layla shot her a look. 'What about your nose?'

Bettina glared.

Ms Stowe eyed the group, her tracksuit glistening in the rain as we stood about her like drowned rats. Anouschka Vosnesensky had a raindrop dangling on the end of her nose.

'So you all want to be models?' Ms Stowe spat. 'You want to get paid just for being pretty? Fancy your chances? Malaika?'

Her eyes zeroed in on Malaika, who shook her head, stung with embarrassment at being singled out. Ms Stowe's lips pursed. Bettina bit gleefully on her bottom lip.

'Go then!' Ms Stowe snorted. 'If you want to be a model, go! Get the hell out of my sight and stop wasting my time.'

The summer rain was sheeting now, almost sizzling as it hit the hot tarmac of the court. Everyone hung their heads. They all badly wanted to make the team. Me? I was only in it for the distraction. But the full force of Ms Stowe's anger was terrifying nonetheless.

'No one?' she seethed. Her face seemingly impenetrable to the rain.

Heads shook nervously.

'Fine,' Ms Stowe said, swapping players over and muddling up the teams, then stalking to the side of the court. 'I don't want to hear anything more about it. Believe me,' she added, 'not one of you is good enough for distractions. Mess about in this game and you're out. Then you can go and model all you like.'

We all slunk back on to the court, heads bowed. I dried my soaking hands on my wet skirt.

'Focus!' Ms Stowe shouted.

Over by the main building, the line of umbrellas was getting shorter. I wondered who'd been selected. I wondered what kind of taste Margot de Souza had. I hoped she liked Emmeline, with her haughty beauty. Rollo was a shoo-in – he was one of the best-looking boys in the school. If Ezra were here, he'd definitely be in.

The game progressed, wet and panicky. The fear of losing out on a place in the team meant everyone made stupid mistakes. I was tired and wanted to go home.

Then I heard some murmuring, and caught a glint of sequins. Anouschka gasped.

Margot de Souza was standing courtside with her assistant, Coco and the headmaster. They had clearly paused to watch on their way back to the helicopter.

My lapse in attention was enough for Bettina to get the ball. Once she had it, she was unstoppable. She shot. She scored. Ms Stowe blew a furious whistle to mark the end of the game.

'For Christ's sake, Norah. Where's your killer instinct?' Ms Stowe shouted. 'Warm down. Go home. I've had enough of you all.'

Bettina affected a catwalk strut to get her water bottle for the benefit of Margot de Souza's gaze. The headmaster was busy pointing out the polo fields and the lavender garden, but the fashionista wasn't listening.

'Shorter in person, isn't she?' Malaika whispered, nodding at Margot de Souza.

I dried my face on my rain-soaked T-shirt. Malaika had some dry tracksuit bottoms in a plastic bag and two KitKats. She chucked me one. I was fixated on Margot de Souza's dress, drinking in the detail to tell my mum when I got home.

'It's an interesting face, isn't it André?' Margot de Souza said in her nasal drawl.

I looked up. They were both staring at Malaika who had momentarily frozen at the attention, tracksuit bottoms half on.

The assistant, André, was nodding and tapping something into his iPad. 'Beautiful,' he agreed, sizing Malaika up with his gaze. 'Sensational eyes.'

Bettina stood at her full height, clearly trying to get noticed too.

'Darling,' called Margot de Souza to Malaika. 'Could we have a word?'

I could see the sudden dazzle in Malaika's eyes, as if she'd known that they'd want her. She finished pulling on her tracksuit bottoms and trotted over.

Coco looked thunderous, as if this was spoiling her plan. She'd clearly envisaged a hand-picked crew, complete with all her BFFs. Malaika was a spanner in the works.

Coco needn't have worried. Before long Malaika was ambling back again, a cocky little grin on her face and a business card in her hand.

'Did they offer it to you?' I asked.

'Yeah, but I said it wasn't for me,' she said.

I was incredulous. 'You turned them down?'

'I told you, I don't have the time allocation,' she said with a huge grin. Clearly all the high she needed was the knowledge of being selected.

I grabbed my wet kit and followed Malaika off the court and on to the path, passing Margot de Souza, who was watching Malaika mournfully.

'A real shame,' she murmured.

The headmaster was anxious to continue the tour. 'Shall we move on to the manicured gardens?' he said.

'You there,' said Margot suddenly. 'Wait!'

Layla, who was just ahead of us, stopped and turned.

'No.' Margot shook her head and Layla scowled. 'The other one.'

I pointed to myself. 'Me?' I said in disbelief.

'Yes, you,' said Margot de Souza. 'Turn around.'

I turned around, self-conscious, everyone looking. My ponytail was dripping with water and I knew my cheeks had to be red. Maybe the rain had been a good thing – stripping us all down to our base essentials.

'She's nice,' said André. 'Earthy.'

I frowned. Coco looked horrified.

Margot de Souza was nodding, the stuffed bird on her hat wobbling with the movement. 'She'd be a good fit. Very girl-next-door.'

'Quite,' agreed André, peering at me over his glasses.

I felt myself blushing crimson under the scrutiny. I didn't think about how awful it would be to go away with Coco, or that our family had been dragged through the press enough already. Or even that they had seen straight to the heart of my ordinariness, because surely that was what girl-next-door really meant. Instead I grinned like an idiot.

The headmaster inspected me, as if struggling to see what they were seeing. There was some hushed conversation. Coco looked like she was about to explode.

Margot came closer. 'What's your name, darling?'

'Norah Whittaker,' I stammered.

Coco interrupted. 'I thought it had all been decided!'

'Margot really wanted a girl-next-door,' André murmured, tapping my name into his iPad.

I felt a rebellious bubble of excitement. Margot de Souza had picked me.

Then Coco shouted, almost in a wail, 'But her dad's in PRISON!'

My whole body curled in on itself. The shame of it hit me red-hot and burning. I never talked about my dad at school. The pain and humiliation was too stark a contrast to the gilded lives at Chelsea High. It gave people like Coco too much ammunition. It was my worst nightmare. Everyone stopped still. I saw Malaika look down at the ground, embarrassed.

Coco looked momentarily panicked at having lost her cool. Margot de Souza frowned.

Then the headmaster, always fearful if someone from the Summers family was upset – they were huge Chelsea High donors – decided that his best course of action was to verify Coco's account.

'Yes, it is worth noting that Norah's father is currently, er . . .' He considered how best to phrase it. '*Serving time* at Her Majesty's pleasure.'

I found myself saying, 'I've got to go.'

Face flaming, I ran away. I actually ran.

Sometimes it's just too hard to stand up tall and take it.

CHAPTER SIX

At the weekend it was raining again. A constant tap tap at my window as I lay on my bed talking to Ezra. With the phone propped up on my pillow it was like we were lying side by side. It was early morning for him and he was all gorgeously mussed hair and eyes hooded from sleep.

I told him all about the auditions and Margot de Souza at the netball court.

'I can't believe you ran away.' He shook his head, exasperated with me.

'I was still cringing when Margot's assistant jogged after me waving a business card. I could barely listen to what he was saying . . . stuff like, "Margot has no prejudice about parents in jail" and I was just trying to shush him.' I went pink just thinking about it.

'But that's amazing, Norah,' Ezra said, pride in his eyes. 'She obviously really liked you.'

I shook my head. 'They just want an average girl-next-door.'

He waved that away like I was fishing for compliments. 'Shut up!'

'It's true!'

'Whatever.' He grinned.

I lay with my head on my arm and stared at his smiling eyes. 'That's enough about me. I've just been blathering on. What's going on there?'

'I like listening to you blather on.'

'So you admit I blather,' I said.

'Norah.' He leaned closer to the screen and whispered with an all-knowing smile, 'Your blather is one of the things I love about you.'

I let my fingers touch the screen, trace the contours of his face. He lifted his hand to meet mine. Skin touching somewhere in cyberspace.

'Oh,' Ezra added. 'Josh wants to show you something.'

He walked with the phone into his brother's room, where Josh was propped up in bed with a giant Lego Millennium Falcon on the covers in front of him. The only giveaway that all wasn't right was the IV cannula in the back of his hand.

'You didn't finish it?' I gasped.

Josh nodded, all proud. 'I did.'

I'd noticed in New York that Ezra always stood slightly away from Josh, afraid of touching him maybe, in case something else went wrong. So I'd feigned a childhood love of Lego, and had insisted we all spend a couple of hours helping Josh build the starship.

'You have to be normal,' I'd warned Ezra before I left. 'He's just a kid. If you tiptoe around him, he'll feel like he's being punished.'

Now, as I admired Josh's Lego handiwork, I was relieved to see Ezra ruffling his hair.

'I wish you were still here, Norah,' Josh said. 'My brother's *way* happier when you are.'

Ezra looked suddenly bashful, maybe embarrassed, as he walked me out of the room.

'Bye, Norah!' Josh sing-songed in the background.

I bit my lip to stop the beaming smile beneath the surface. Ezra started to say something, the tips of his cheekbones slightly pink from a blush.

It was then that my door flew open and my mum was there, work laptop resting open on her forearm. 'Norah, we've got to go – Oh . . .' She paused. 'Sorry. I thought you were doing your homework?'

'I was,' I said, and knew that I'd inadvertently made talking to Ezra sound like a disturbance.

My mum was clearly annoyed. She'd had a bee in her bonnet about homework since parents' evening, when she discovered I hadn't done any since Dad went to prison. I think bringing it up helped her feel like she had some control somewhere in life.

'I'd better go,' I said to Ezra.

He grinned. 'See ya.'

'I love you,' I said as quietly as I could, conscious that my mum was still in the doorway.

'Me too,' he replied and hung up.

I looked at my mum. 'Happy now?'

'Ecstatic,' she replied, all sarcasm as she typed one-handed on her laptop. Then she sighed. 'Norah, I understand what's going on between you and Ezra. And I think it's lovely, I really do. I just wonder if it has to be so serious.'

I frowned. I didn't want to hear anything negative about one of the most important relationships in my life right then. My main source of happiness.

'I just don't want you to put all your eggs in one basket,' Mum said, leaning against my doorframe. 'You're on the phone to him all the time. You don't know when he's coming back, and I don't want you sitting around waiting for him, missing out on other things.'

I listened, fury rising as she spoke as if she were the world expert in relationships. I wanted to say, 'What, like with you and Dad?' but I didn't.

The angry silence that hung in the air was a sign of how distant we'd become.

My mum sighed. 'Your grandparents will be here soon,' she said, then left the room.

Today was visiting day. My call to Ezra had actually been to take my mind off that fact. We usually visited Dad separately from my grandparents, but they were heading off on an exclusive cruise of the Galapagos Islands the next day – 'Following in Darwin's footsteps, darling' – and wanted to see my dad before they left. There was a three-person limit on visiting, so my granddad would wait in the car, which suited him fine. It was clear how much the prison visits affected him. He was constantly ringing my mum to inform her of the new avenues he was pushing the lawyers to explore, anything to try and shorten my dad's sentence and put an end to the horror.

Today's visiting dynamic was not ideal, because Mum didn't really see eye to eye with her in-laws. This meant one of our precious two one-hour visits a month would be extra awkward.

At one o'clock sharp, my grandparents rapped on the door. My mum was downing coffee while trying to deal with a work crisis email from one of the fabric factories in Bangladesh. I was eating a sandwich while staring blankly at my biology textbook. I wore the jeans and bright blue T-shirt that I kept for prison visits. I couldn't wear them any other time.

I hadn't made the team for that weekend's netball game. Malaika had gone as reserve.

I let my grandparents in. My grandmother was dressed neatly in a beige twill skirt and cream silk blouse with a ruffle at the neck. She wore her bag hanging in the crook of her arm like the Queen. She'd have made an excellent member of the royal family – very discreet, no overt emotion.

'Hello, Norah darling. All ready?'

I nodded, mouth full of sandwich.

My granddad followed down the steps behind her, dressed

in his customary chinos and blazer. He always stooped when he entered, but it was all psychological because there was plenty of room for him to stand up straight on the boat. He just couldn't fathom how people survived in such a small space. That's what happens when you've always been rich.

'Is your phone working properly?' he asked as he came in and stood awkwardly by the bookcase. Much to my mum's horror, they'd bought me a new iPhone so they could keep in touch better. My granddad thinks money solves everything.

'Yeah, it's great thanks,' I said, pulling my trainers on.

'Do you need anything else?' my grandmother asked.

'No she doesn't!' my mum shouted from the kitchen counter without looking up from her email.

'Oh, hello, Lois,' my grandmother called, then to me said more quietly, 'Your granddad thought you might need a laptop for school.'

My mum slid off the bar stool and chucked her work phone in her bag. 'She doesn't need a laptop, Evelyn. They have laptops at school. And she has the iPad you got her for Christmas.'

I silently prayed they wouldn't mention the new bike they'd bought me as well. A couple of months ago the crank on my old Peugeot racer had rusted straight through on my way to their house, making the pedal fall off and tumbling me into a gold-plated Lamborghini cruising down Knightsbridge. My granddad declared the bike a deathtrap, had it scrapped, and bought me a new one. I hadn't dared tell my mum – either about the accident, so as not to worry her, or the new bike, so as not to really annoy her.

It was enough for my mum that we were indebted to my grandparents for the lawyers and the boat berth. We might be broke, but she didn't want to take a single penny more from them than she had to. That was why I locked my new bike up at the top of the jetty, so she never knew it was mine.

As my mum put her raincoat on, my granddad was saying, 'We just think a laptop would be better for Norah's academic work, and we don't want her to miss out because her father is . . .'

'In jail?' my mum said as Granddad looked for more discreet terminology.

'Incarcerated,' he said. 'Yes.'

'She's not missing out, Roger.' My mum ushered us all out of the boat, keys jangling in her hand. She hated talking about money. We were here because of Dad's mistakes. I knew without having to ask that she wanted to be back on Mulberry Island, where no one cared about who had what. 'Norah has everything she could possibly need. A lot more, probably. And I'm working full-time so we have plenty of money.'

My grandmother looked uncertain about this as we filed out into the summer drizzle: me with my hood up, her with her brolly, my granddad in his panama hat. But my mum closed the subject by looking at her watch and saying, 'We need to hurry or we'll be late, and this is the highlight of Bill's life.'

My grandparents' butler, Harold, usually drove them everywhere. But today my granddad was behind the wheel of the Bentley. I think driving took his mind off where we were going.

'Do you want to sit up front, Norah?' he asked.

I climbed in the passenger seat. I like talking to Granddad. It's easier when Mum's not there because I can feel her judging me on our subject matter: sport, dogs, the weather.

'Did you make the team?' he asked as he pulled out into the oncoming traffic like he owned the road.

'Not this time.'

From the back seat, Mum said, 'What team?'

I didn't get to answer because her phone rang. It was her boss with more supply problems.

My grandmother peered forward between the front seats. 'Should she be working on a Saturday?' she asked me.

I shrugged. 'If you need shirts, it doesn't matter what day it is.'

She wrinkled her nose, unhappy with the state of affairs. When Mum hung up, she said, 'Lois, this all looks very stressful for you. Please let us help you out . . .'

Mum held up a hand. 'Evelyn, as I've said before, that's a very kind offer, but we don't need any money. Now it's a long drive, so if we're going to get there without arguing, let's not mention it again.' Then she rested her head on her scrunched-up cardigan against the car door and fell asleep.

Me and my grandparents made small talk about the inclement summer weather and the upcoming church fete where the WI were in charge of making cakes.

'I am a terrible baker,' my grandmother confessed. 'Roger always makes them for me. He does the most wonderful lemon drizzle, don't you, Roger?'

'I can whip up an exceedingly light sponge,' Granddad agreed. 'Voted best bake two years in a row.'

The old Victorian jail building loomed up like something out of a horror film, with broken windows, barbed wire and pigeons nesting on the roof. Everywhere were signs, warnings, check boxes, all locks and chains and drear. The rain didn't help.

When the Bentley pulled up in the car park, a woman getting out of the van next to us slammed the door so hard my mum woke up with a start – 'Jesus!' – and held her hand to her chest in surprise. When she saw where we were, I watched her exhale long and slow. She got out her mirror and checked her make-up.

My granddad relayed a hundred questions that he wanted my grandmother to ask.

'I'll just tell Bill you love him,' my grandmother scolded. 'That's all he wants to know.'

Granddad nodded, chastened, then got his newspaper out to settle down to wait.

We headed to the visitors' hall. Most of our possessions had to be locked away, apart from money for the dreadful vending-machine coffee. We could leave certain gifts in a box. I'd brought my dad a book on the history of cinema, and my mum had got him socks and pants – Hudson and Sons samples from work. My grandmother had got him socks too – cashmere ones from Harrods.

My mum started looking for her ID. My grandmother of course had hers ready. I had my passport. The woman on duty didn't smile at my mum as she madly rifled through her bag saying, 'It's here somewhere!' My mum always gets nervous at these visits. You never get used to them.

The search scanner was broken, so we had to be searched physically. We stood in line, barefoot. There was something stupid and humiliating about having to hold your shoes. When they frisked us, I tried to pretend I was at the airport, but it never worked. The guard ran her hands along my arms, down my legs, around the inside of my jeans waistband, never once looking me in the eye. I felt instantly guilty, like it was me that'd done something wrong.

'They brought a bloody sniffer dog in to my queue!' My grandmother was horrified. 'The *indignity*. It's appalling.'

That seemed to cheer Mum up a bit. She hid it, but I could tell.

The smell in the visitors' hall hit me straight away. Medicinal like a hospital – antiseptic masking something darker underneath, cold and pungent. It wasn't people dying here, but hope. When we first read the visitors' information we'd had a laugh over the dress code – 'Both breasts must be covered'. We didn't laugh any more.

The visitors' hall was a giant room with a scuffed blue laminate floor, rows of white tables and black chairs. There were cracks in the plaster on the ceiling and bars on windows higher up than anyone could reach. Guards watched, hands behind their backs.

Other visitors were already in place. A red-eyed old man was listening as his wife told him a long story about their dog. A black guy watched his toddler play with the prison toys. A really young white guy was having a hushed argument with his tired-looking girlfriend, while an Eastern European couple were laughing hysterically about something, almost treating the place like home.

Dad looked small and old and alone, his skin an unhealthy grey. I noticed that his face had hardened since our last visit. Would he be all sharp corners soon? How long would his soft jollity withhold? But then he spotted us and his face lit up.

My mum looked so sadly happy when she saw him that I thought she might cry.

It's strange having a time limit on chat. The ticking clock infuses everyone with a sense of panic. Small talk feels like wasted time, like we should just be discussing big stuff – but big stuff feels too serious, and if there's an argument of any sort it's a disaster.

Dad said, 'Look at you. Growing up so fast,' all wistful, even though he'd only seen me a fortnight ago. 'How was America? How's Ezra?'

I told him about New York, though I could tell my grandmother was itching to ask questions. The dynamic was so unnatural, so forced, that it was impossible to get close to normal.

My grandmother pursed her lips. 'You've lost weight and you're a bit pale, Bill. Are there enough vegetables?'

I could tell Dad wanted just ten minutes alone with Mum. 'Shall we go and get a coffee, Gran?' I suggested.

An argument broke out between the Eastern European couple, which the guards attempted to shut down. My grandmother flinched at the shouting.

Sitting at one table was a man I hadn't seen before: well turned out with glossy black hair and greying sideburns. He looked completely out of place, like he should be in a suit at a gentleman's club. He was being visited by a smooth young guy, maybe his son, maybe an employee. A sharp click of this man's fingers silenced the arguing couple quicker than the guards.

He tipped his head as my grandmother passed, half getting out of his seat. 'Good morning.'

Gran looked a little flustered by the attention. 'Morning,' she stuttered.

The hushed chat between my parents stopped the minute we came back.

Dad plastered on a smile. 'So, Norah honey, what's going on this term? Fill me in.'

'Inter-School Sports Tournament and the Variety Performance,' I said, not that desperate to talk about school. I was more interested to know what my parents had been discussing.

'God, I loved the Variety Performance,' my dad reminisced. 'Only reason to go to school.'

My grandmother clucked like he was a bad influence on me.

'I was Curly in Oklahoma,' he carried on, ignoring her. 'Remember, Lois? *Oh the corn is as high as an elephant's eye* . . .' he started to sing and his eyes misted up with the memory. 'What were you, Lois?'

Mum dismissed the question. 'Oh, I can't remember.'

My mum never acknowledged the fact she'd ever performed, as if it were a silliness she'd grown out of. My dad on the other hand would take that passion to his grave. That addiction to the stage ran through my veins too. As a really little kid, I'd felt my fingers tingle as I watched him audition. First chance I had, I was up there beside him, reeling off lines with precocious flamboyance. Then, over time, I settled down and relaxed into the roles, realised that less was more, and actually got a good role in one of the low-budget films my dad

45

was involved in. It was all so exciting – before the fraudulent financing came to light.

'Of course you can remember! What was it?' My dad was animated, truly engaged for the first time since we'd arrived. 'You were Judy Garland. I remember. *Somewhere Over the Rainbow*! You wore a blue shimmery dress and red stilettos. The headmaster thought your outfit was too risqué. How could I possibly have forgotten?'

My mum smiled gently, humouring him. 'Oh yes, of course.'

'It's all coming back now,' Dad said, leaning forward. 'Remember Titus Summers? He was Frank Sinatra. Thought he was all cool in his suit and hat, but couldn't hit a note. His voice broke an hour before he went on, rotten timing, and he had to speak half the lines. What an idiot. You must remember that, Lois?'

'I remember,' my mum said tightly, like she wanted to do anything but.

'We were in hysterics in the wing.' Dad grinned with delight. 'Titus was furious!'

I knew that my parents and Coco's mum and dad had gone to school together, but it was still weird to imagine it. But as my dad chuckled away, nothing else mattered except that sound. I'd forgotten what it was like to see him laugh.

'So you're auditioning?' Dad said. 'For the Variety Show?'

I screwed up my face. 'Not this year.'

'Why not?' He was confused, incredulous.

'I just don't really want to,' I said more quietly, unable to look him in the eye.

'You must!'

'Don't push her, Bill,' Mum warned.

'I'm not pushing her!'

'I am playing netball in the Sports Tournament,' I cut in, wanting to quell the tension.

My dad shuddered.

'Darling, there's nothing wrong with a bit of netball,' my grandmother said. 'I was a very good wing attack in my day.'

Dad looked uninspired. 'I'm just not a fan of organised sport. It's like a religion. All too much group mentality. Bit like in here, actually.'

My mum raised a brow. 'Bill, you can't compare netball to prison.'

He shrugged like he definitely could. 'Just promise you won't become a jock, Norah.'

I shook my head, relieved at the softening of the atmosphere. 'I won't.'

The status quo returned. Coffees were sipped and the disgustingness agreed upon.

Then my grandmother said, 'I've put some money on your card, Bill.'

'Thanks, Mum.'

'I've tried to get Lois to take some but –'

'Don't, Evelyn!' Mum snapped.

Dad's brow furrowed deep.

My grandmother looked all harassed. 'Well, I'm just trying to –'

'Evelyn!' Mum cut her off.

Dad looked worried now. 'Are you short of money, Lois? Maybe you should –'

My mum cut him off too. 'Bill, don't!'

My grandmother's lips tightened. She crossed her arms over her chest, eyes a little watery – overwhelmed. My mum's jaw was set. I sank lower in my chair.

The Eastern European couple shouted again and my grandmother jumped in her seat. My mum glared at a flickering strip light. The baby behind us started really crying. Bawling, ear-splitting wails as his mum tried with no success to shush him. The baby's dad got cross.

My dad looked panicked, trying to think of ways to make the atmosphere better. The clock was ticking. We only had fifteen minutes left.

I found myself saying, 'I got selected for a modelling competition. On a Greek island. For Vox.'

My dad's mouth started to smile again.

'Vox?' said Mum sharply. 'As in *the* Vox?'

I nodded.

'With Margot de Souza?' she asked, almost disbelieving.

I nodded again.

'Bloody hell, Norah. You didn't tell me this!'

My dad had gone all starry-eyed. 'Will you be on TV? I could get everyone here to watch it. We'd have a premiere.' He didn't care about the netball. He cared about the bright lights of fame. 'This is so exciting. My daughter, a star!'

'Hang on,' I said, worried he was getting carried away. 'I'm not sure I'm going to do it.'

His face fell. 'Why not?'

'It's with Coco,' I said, which was enough of an explanation as far as I was concerned. I couldn't tell him that I had run away as soon as his jail term was mentioned. It had been a clear error of judgement to mention it at all.

Dad frowned. 'Norah, this is a huge opportunity. You can't let Coco Summers spoil your fun.'

How little my dad knew about my life.

'How much are they paying you?' Mum queried.

I told her and her eyes widened.

Then my grandmother said tersely, 'So you'll take Norah's money.'

My mum looked set to blow. 'How could you– even – '

I couldn't believe we were here again – everyone furious. The guard shouted, 'Ten minutes!' And I found myself saying . . .

'I suppose I could do it.'

My dad's eyes lifted, hopeful. Suddenly he was on his feet. 'Hey, Benji, get this – my daughter's going to be on TV!'

The Eastern European guy looked up. 'Nice,' he said, thumbs up with approval.

The well-groomed man who'd impressed my grandmother suddenly looked up. 'What's this?' he asked.

Dad looked amazed that he'd sparked the man's interest. 'Vincent,' he stammered. 'This is my daughter, Norah. She's going to be in a Vox commercial.'

The man's lips curved. 'Congratulations, young lady.'

I almost thought he was going to click his fingers and order champagne. I blushed at the attention.

Lowering his voice, my dad said, 'That's Vincent Blake!' As if we should have heard about him. 'Big news around here. Virtually runs the place. Never spoken to me before. He has Cuban cigars flown in!'

'How does he manage that?' my grandmother asked.

'They drone them in through the broken windows.'

My grandmother looked horrified. 'Surely that's not allowed.'

'It's the least of their problems.' My dad laughed, the ins and outs of prison life now his norm.

A fight broke out at the other end of the hall and the guards carted one of the guys off. Ignoring it, Dad said, 'So what are you doing tonight? Wow me with tales of the outside world.'

'Working,' my mum said.

'Homework,' I said, regretfully.

My dad made a face like both those answers were rubbish. 'And you, Mum?'

'Dinner at the Savoy with the Obrechts,' said Gran. 'Do

you remember their son, Toby? You were great chums at school. Just bought a catamaran apparently. Enormous great thing. Going to sail round the world.'

My dad forced a smile. He never used to care about things like Toby Obrecht's success. But now he had fallen so far, it felt like everything worked to highlight his failures.

'Five minutes,' the guard called.

Around us people were getting up to leave. The baby was still crying.

'I can't wait to see your advert, Norah,' Dad said. 'That's really given me something to look forward to.'

There was no going back now. I'd do anything, even surrender myself to Coco and her fawning entourage, to give him that small slice of happiness. A bit of hope.

As we got up to leave, Vincent Blake said, 'Good luck with your advertisement, Norah.' Then to my grandmother he said slickly, 'I'd recommend the turbot wellington at the Savoy. Always a favourite of mine.'

Gran was so taken aback by his charm, she tittered. Which made the rest of us laugh.

Vincent Blake was clearly pleased with the reaction. 'You've got a delightful family there, Bill,' he said.

I watched as my dad's stooped shoulders straightened at Vincent's comment and he puffed out his chest with pride.

CHAPTER SEVEN

After a prison visit, I always rang my friend Jess on Mulberry Island. We'd been inseparable when we lived a walk away from one another. Now it was harder to keep in touch with school and the distance, especially as I daren't set foot on the island any more. But we'd made a pact that I would ring her every time I'd been to see Dad.

Jess knew I didn't talk about it with anyone else. I might have with Ezra, but if I was honest, I wasn't that keen on pushing home the differences between us. While my dad was languishing in prison, Ezra's was an uber-wealthy financial consultant. And yes, deep down, I was ashamed. So I called Jess instead. And even with her, I didn't dwell on it for too long.

'How was it?'

'Hideous.'

She laughed. I told her about the Vox advert.

'Oh my god, Norah, you *have* to do it! I would *love* to be in a Vox advert!' Coming from Jess, who hadn't the least interest in fashion or make-up, that was saying something.

I stared out of the window of the boat. 'Well, I have to now.

My dad's going to have the whole prison watching.'

'He'll probably sell tickets,' she joked. But it was a bit too close to the bone and I couldn't come up with a witty reply quick enough to cover the fact. The second of silence had her saying, 'Sorry.'

'It's fine,' I said quickly.

I know I handle things in a very roundabout way. After the first ever prison visit, Jess had said, 'It's OK to cry, Norah.' But I'd said, 'No it's not.' Because me and Mum had to keep this together for Dad. We weren't allowed to break down.

The next morning, Jess had asked me to meet her in Leicester Square. It was the Christmas holidays and icy sleet froze our faces as we met at the Tube.

'We're going to the cinema,' she told me. '*The Notebook*'s on and I really want to see it. It's a silver screening.'

'We can't go to a silver screening,' I said with a laugh as we walked into the warm foyer of the Odeon. 'It's for old people.'

'We can. I checked. And we get a cup of tea.' For Jess that was a prize in itself.

'Why do you want to see *The Notebook*?' I asked as she bought the tickets. 'Isn't it really sad?'

And then I realised what she was doing.

I wanted to walk away but she'd already paid. Anyway, I knew she wouldn't let me off that easily. So I followed her into the half-empty screen, and over a bucket of sweet popcorn and a cup of tea, for an hour and a half in the darkness of the cinema, I cried my eyes out.

CHAPTER EIGHT

Coco was away from school most of the following week, promoting the Vox Midsummer perfume overseas in the lead up to the launch. Her constant selfies with fans in various department stores worldwide became so grating that by the middle of the week even Daniel had muted her on Instagram.

Against my every instinct, I'd called Vox to say that I would be interested in being part of the commercial. They were delighted – they could tick 'girl-next-door' off their list of criteria. Along with Coco, as far as I knew, the rest of the group going were Rollo, Emmeline, Verity, Freddie, Emir, Ned and Yannis. No surprises there. They were all the beautiful people – that's why they were friends.

Since Mum's comments, Ezra and I had spoken less but messaged more, which in my opinion was more distracting because I stopped doing homework every time my phone vibrated.

Since telling her I was doing the modelling, Ms Stowe was even harder on me at netball. She set me extra training, giving me an excuse not to have to hang out on the boat with my mum. It was quite enjoyable to be out jogging beside the river after school. I crossed Battersea Bridge and wove my way round Battersea Park, finishing at the Peace Pagoda, where I did some sprints up and down the steps, ending up sweaty and exhausted.

'Hey, Norah!'

Freddie Chang was wearing a tux, hands in the pockets of his black trousers. 'That's far too energetic for this time in the evening,' he said, strolling up from the river.

I stopped what I was doing, conscious of my red-faced appearance as the rest of the polo team sidled over looking equally dressed up. Emir was on the phone. Ned was scoffing a hamburger, while Yannis glugged down a Coke. I didn't know the rest of the team that well – they were just the type of people everyone knew *about*.

'Where are you going?' I asked as the evening sun glinted on the water.

'Some polo dinner,' said Yannis dismissively. I'd had a Maths detention with him once. He was always friendly. Tall and thin with dark-rimmed glasses. Olive skin, eyes like he was wearing layers of liner. 'They're auctioning off a lesson with Laurent.'

On cue, Laurent Summers appeared from behind one of the bushes, white shirt half unbuttoned, his arm slung around a giggling girl I vaguely recognised from the year above. Their hair was all tousled, like they'd just got out of bed. They paused when they reached the rest of the group and Laurent peered at me over the top of his sunglasses.

'What's going on here?' he said.

The girl eyed my sweaty red face with displeasure. She was wearing a little black dress and heels, and the jacket of Laurent's tux was draped over her shoulders.

'Waiting for you,' said Yannis, slightly exasperated.

Laurent grinned, pushing his aviators back up his nose. Doing a mock bow, he said, 'Lead the way, sir.'

'OK, let's go,' Yannis called, impatient.

Ned and Emir sauntered off.

Freddie grinned. 'See you, Norah.'

I raised a hand and was about to jog off in the opposite direction when Freddie's grin widened.

'Looks like Coco and Ezra are having fun in New York, eh?' he said.

My pulse quickened faster than it had on any of the sprints. 'What?'

'Come on!' Yannis shouted, several paces ahead.

Freddie bounded away. 'Thought you knew,' he called over his shoulder, face alight from the thrill of delivering great gossip.

As soon as they were out of sight, I sat down on the pagoda steps and got my phone out. Unmuting Coco's Instagram, I didn't even need to scroll through her feed. There at the top was a picture of her and Ezra eating pizza in a cosy little place in Chinatown. The best pizza in New York, apparently. We hadn't been able to get a table when I was there.

Adrenaline pumping, I immediately phoned Ezra.

'Hey,' he said. It was mid-afternoon there, and I could hear traffic in the background.

'I can't believe you were with Coco and didn't tell me,' I said, my heart pounding.

'What –'

My brain was racing ahead of itself. The two of them cosying up after their pizza, walking hand in hand through Central Park . . . 'Why didn't you tell me? I had to hear it from Freddie Chang!'

'Hang on a minute.' I could hear the annoyance in Ezra's voice.

The adrenaline was fading. I felt my brain get muddled. I said, a bit quieter, 'Why didn't you tell me you saw Coco?'

'Jesus Christ,' Ezra muttered. 'Are you serious?'

'Yes,' I said. 'I can't believe you didn't tell me.'

I heard him exhale. 'We literally just had lunch. She wanted to see Josh. She's known him since he was baby, Norah.'

I felt stupid. Small. 'Oh.'

There was silence. There was never silence. I wanted to take it back.

'Sorry, I should have . . .'

'Don't worry about it.' He sighed. 'Look, things are not good here.'

The tone of his voice made me sit up straighter. 'What's happened?'

'Some bloody new surgeon thinks Josh's operation's too risky.'

'What?' Risky wasn't a word you wanted to hear when talking about operating on a ten-year-old. 'But the other guy was really positive.'

'Yeah, so who do you believe?' Ezra sounded tense, angry.

'Oh shit. I'm really sorry.' And there I'd been accusing him of having pizza with Coco. I squeezed my eyes shut, feeling awful. 'Ezra, what can I do?'

'Nothing. Look, I've gotta go, my mum's just turned up, she had another meeting at the hospital.'

'OK,' I said, biting my lip. 'Listen, I'm sorry about before.'

'Seriously, don't worry about it,' he said, voice distracted.

And we hung up.

CHAPTER NINE

When I finally got back to the boat, I could barely put one foot in front of the other. I had made myself do the most punishing run home as payback for my over-reactive phone call. My legs were on fire, my throat parched, and my skin was radiating heat and glossy with sweat.

Mum looked horrified when I staggered through the door. She came rushing over from where she was doing the washing-up. 'Norah, what have you done to yourself?'

I weakly waved her attention away. I could taste the copper tang of blood in my mouth. 'Water. Just need water,' I panted, collapsing on the sofa.

Mum fetched me a glass. 'Thanks,' I stammered, gulping it down then feeling sick.

'What's going on?' she pushed, anxiously hovering over me.

'Ezra saw Coco in New York and didn't tell me, and I rang him and now he's angry with me,' I blurted out.

I immediately regretted my words, considering her opinion of Ezra. But she just sighed, 'Oh, Norah,' all sweet pity.

She had her hair down, all wavy and relaxed, and was wearing her yoga leggings and a soft white sweatshirt. She had a cup of coffee on the kitchen counter which she grabbed. Then she sat next to me, putting her arm round my shoulders.

I felt tears well up in my eyes. The sweat was drying on my body and I started to shiver. I waited for her to say, 'I told you so,' but instead she said:

'Honey, the thing about relationships is you have to trust the other person. Otherwise there's no point.'

I looked at her, surprised.

She smiled. 'You can't assume just because Coco was with him that anything happened.' She pushed my sweaty hair out of my eyes. 'Look at the state you're in. If you do this every time there's a problem, you're going to drive yourself mad. For goodness' sake, the guy's told you he loves you. At least allow him the benefit of the doubt!'

I felt myself staring up at her like a child. 'I thought you said we shouldn't be so serious as a couple,' I said, my voice a bit muffled by her jumper.

'No. I said don't put everything into it and leave yourself with nothing else.'

I started to shiver again. She held me tight, pulling the crocheted blanket down from the back of the sofa and wrapping it round me.

'But I can see that it's probably too late for that,' she said, looking heavenward. She offered me her coffee. I wrapped my hands round the warmth of the mug and took a big gulp.

'Relationships are complicated, hey?' she said, her hand stroking my hair. She took the coffee back and put it on the table. 'Let me tell you something my mum used to say.'

I knew very little about my mum's mum, except that she'd been married five times and lived on a yacht. I'd gleaned all that from a tabloid newspaper because my mum never talked about her. I was surprised she was bringing her up now.

She straightened the blanket round my shoulders. 'When I was a little girl, my mum said, "Now, Lois, just remember. True love does not conquer all and there are no happy ever afters. No one believes in fairies so why the hell do they believe in fairy tales?"' She gave me a look to suggest only a mother like hers could say such a thing.

I made a face. 'That's not very hopeful.'

'Well,' said my mum, 'I used to agree with you. But on the other hand, more and more, Norah, I'm starting to understand it. It's *you* that's in control. It's not fate or destiny or what's "meant to be". Relationships are hard work. You have to fight for them. You work at them because someone is worth the effort.'

I thought about Ezra, about when I would reach out and touch his hand on the screen. I thought about my dad, alone in his cell. I toyed with the crochet flowers on the blanket. I could smell Mum's perfume, her skin.

Mum gave me a gentle nudge. 'Go and have a shower – a

quick one, remember, because water costs money – and then call him back. You'll feel much better after that.'

I nodded. Smiled. 'Thanks, Mum.'

I FaceTimed Ezra sitting on my bed in my pyjamas. 'I was just jealous,' I said when he answered, picking at the bobbles of wool on the blanket on my bed. Outside a pleasure cruiser went past, gently rocking the boat.

Ezra ran his hands through his thick dark hair. 'I know Coco can be a pain. But it was just quite nice to see an old friend, to go for pizza and forget the bad stuff for a while.' He smiled, but it didn't reach his eyes. 'I can't tell you everything I do.'

'I know,' I said, and lay down so I could be close to the screen. It seemed like everyone was softening to Coco. Like her toxicity was so commonplace people had become immune to it. Or maybe it was just completely different if she liked you.

'What did you talk about?' I asked.

'Coco,' he said, and I laughed. He laughed too.

I scrunched up his hockey sweatshirt to rest my head on. 'How's Josh?'

'Not great,' Ezra said, and told me what he knew about the operation.

We didn't talk for long because he had to go to the hospital. I must have fallen asleep almost as soon as we hung up, exhausted from my run. I woke up when my mum came in

63

and put my phone on the shelf under my window, right next to the snow globe Ezra gave me at Christmas. She draped me in my sheet and kissed my forehead.

'All OK?' she asked.

I smiled sleepily. 'All OK.'

CHAPTER TEN

The day had come for us to leave for Greece. I was equal measures excited and dreading it. The island would be magical, but it would also be one long Coco Show.

I was travelling light. Luckily I didn't have to worry about clothes for the commercial, but my brain short-circuited when I tried to work out what to pack for a weekend away with just people from Chelsea High. I stood folding and refolding a red T-shirt and pair of denim shorts in a frozen stupor. One thing I made sure I crammed in my rucksack was Ezra's old Chelsea High hockey sweatshirt. I couldn't sleep without it nowadays.

I messaged him as I waited nervously for the Uber, which was late and struggling to find our boat.

Are you awake? I knew the time in NY off by heart now and it was 2 a.m.

His reply came back almost immediately. *For you I can be.*

I smiled. *You should be asleep.*

You're the one who woke me up!

The taxi appeared. I replied with a bright red heart and felt immediately a little calmer about the trip ahead.

The airport was crazy. We were late and so I ran with my

bag on my back while my mum followed behind, cutting in and out of crowds of people to get to the check-in desk.

It was hard to miss our group. Coco was in the centre, surrounded by suitcases like Venus in her shell, wearing a huge-brimmed sunhat, blue and white striped crop top and tiny white shorts with two rows of brass buttons up the front. Massive dark glasses completed the pretence of trying to be incognito, while people walking past snapped her unsubtly on their phones. Her lips were set in a perfect pout, in anticipation of the paparazzi.

Verity was next to her in a baby-pink baseball cap, baggy pink T-shirt and shimmering cycling shorts. Verity's sister was an infamous influencer, and by association Verity was worth a sly photo or two.

Ned Fitzgibbon was laughing hysterically with Yannis and Emir about something on Yannis's phone. The big polo sports bags they were using for suitcases were piled in a heap in front of them, except for Emir who had Louis Vuitton luggage.

All the Vox people were clucking about, doing harassed last-minute checks. I had to look away when my mum collared André for an embarrassing chaperone talk. Looking around for an ally, I saw only Emmeline snogging Rollo next to a luggage trolley. But then I got a tap on the shoulder. To my delight, Malaika was standing there, dressed in skin-tight jeans and a baggy black T-shirt.

She laughed at my expression. 'Surprise!'

'What are you doing here?'

She shrugged, all cool and nonchalant. 'I figured, why not?'

Her dad appeared behind her, tall and slick in his suit, same big, almond-shaped eyes as Malaika. 'That's not strictly true is it?' he said, with a wry smile. Then to me said, 'I told Malaika that she had misconstrued my advice. Every opportunity that comes one's way is worth grasping.'

Malaika faked a yawn. 'OK, you can leave now,' she said.

Her dad made a face like she'd mortally wounded him. I found myself grinning. I liked Malaika's parents. I had been to their home for dinner once, where their aesthetic was all minimalist Scandi-chic with pops of vibrant textiles. I thought how nice it would be, under different circumstances, if they were friends with my parents and we could all hang out. It was those moments when I caught myself thinking: why couldn't my dad just *not* have done what he did?

With a quick kiss, a 'Be good', and a wink, Malaika's dad strode off. My mum was still grilling André about the rules and regulations of the trip.

'I'm so pleased you're here,' I said to Malaika.

'I wouldn't have done it if you weren't coming,' Malaika replied, surveying the rest of the crowd. One of Margot de Souza's harassed minions was handing out boarding passes, while another dealt with the bags. André was still being questioned by my mother.

'First class,' said Ned, studying the ticket.

Verity glanced up with a frown. 'Of course.'

'Don't lose these!' the assistant demanded, like we were children.

'No, sir,' mocked Rollo and got a death stare in response. It seemed more like something Freddie would say. I realised then that I hadn't seen Freddie yet.

'Where's your brother?' I asked Emmeline.

Rollo replied, 'He's not coming.'

I wanted to say, 'I asked Emmeline!' Instead I kept my gaze firmly on Emmeline and said, 'Why not?'

Again Rollo answered. 'Banned. Too many Fs.'

'Did they get a replacement?' Malaika asked.

'An upgrade rather than a replacement,' said a voice behind us. Turning, I saw Laurent Summers walking out of WHSmith, biting down on a bar of Dairy Milk, all cocky smirk and twinkling eyes.

'Oh god!' Malaika grimaced.

Laurent grinned, striding past to where Yannis and Emir were sitting on their luggage. 'You love me really.'

My mum came over and gave me a big hug. 'Behave yourself. Don't do anything silly. I'm trusting you, Norah,' she said.

I spotted a patronising little grin on Laurent's face as he chucked a bottle of Cherry Coke to his sister.

'Where's mine?' asked Yannis.

Laurent shrugged.

Yannis shook his head in disbelief. 'I only asked you a minute ago.'

Mum clasped me to her chest again. 'Oh, my baby girl.'

I pushed her off, embarrassed. She looked so forlorn that I gave her another quick hug in apology. 'Will you be OK on your own?' I asked.

'Of course,' she answered. 'Anyway, I have a shipment of maroon V-neck jumpers stuck in customs to deal with. Oh, the glamour!'

'OK, people, let's go!' André clapped his hands to usher us through to departures.

As we got our stuff together, an awkward, greasy-haired girl asked Coco shyly for an autograph. Coco scrawled on her pad and smiled sweetly for a photo. When she thought the girl was out of earshot, Coco added something under her breath to Verity that had them in stitches. I saw the greasy-haired girl turn, then scuttle off head down. I was already regretting the trip, and every minute spent with Coco and her toxic gang.

Mum was waiting at the bag drop-off. She gave a little wave. How easy it would be to run back . . .

But then Malaika appeared by my side, having popped to the loo. 'I can't believe Laurent is here,' she said. 'He's such a dick.'

Ahead of us Laurent drawled, 'I can hear you,' without turning round.

'Good!' Malaika replied with a shake of her head.

'Why don't you like him?' I asked.

Malaika handed her passport over to the woman at the desk. 'A variety of reasons,' she muttered.

I was intrigued to hear the list of grievances. I looked back at my mum for one last wave, but she had her head down, checking her emails.

CHAPTER ELEVEN

I sat next to Malaika on the plane. She gave me the low-down on Laurent while the flight attendant poured orange juice into crystal glasses and took orders from our menus. I hadn't flown anywhere before my trip to New York, and now here I was again – both times in first class. It was surreal.

Malaika had no such worries. She settled down with her blanket. 'Laurent's an idiot,' she informed me. 'Did he really need to go to Argentina for six months? Everyone reckons his dad sent him to split him up with some much older woman he was dating. Apparently she was one of his parents' friends.'

I made a face. 'Really?'

Malaika nodded, expression disparaging. 'I think he's actually a bit crap at polo.'

I snorted into my orange juice and took one of the croissants that the flight attendant was offering.

Malaika's major bugbear with Laurent was that he'd spent most of the previous year trying to split her up with her boyfriend Hugo Caruthers, and nearly succeeded. Sowing little seeds of doubt, saying he'd seen Hugo up to all sorts behind Malaika's back.

'He just made it all up to try and get me to dump Hugo,' said Malaika. She was eating a pain au chocolat while painting her nails acid yellow, making our section of the plane smell toxic. 'All total lies. Hugo's the most honest person I know. And what did Laurent think? That I'd go running into his open arms?' She glanced up at me, one brow raised. 'He's a self-centred fool.'

Laurent was sitting over the other side of the plane, black headphones on, eyes shut. He seemed to sense that we were talking about him and rolled his head our way, opening one eye like a cat keeping a tab on its prey. There was no denying that he was good-looking, with skin that glowed from the Argentinian sun and laughing green eyes. But there was an air about him that you knew you couldn't trust.

Malaika huffed, like he didn't even have the right to look our way.

Behind Laurent, Emmeline was asleep, curled up in the crook of Rollo's arm. Behind Emmeline, Coco and Verity were sniggering about something on Coco's phone. I turned back in my plush seat, sipped my juice and thanked the lord that Malaika had deigned to accept Margot de Souza's invitation.

The flight was three hours. When we ran out of chat, we watched a film and I had a little nap. On landing, we stepped out of the plane into balmy Greek heat, palm trees in the distance, a mirage shimmering on the tarmac. For the first time, I was one hundred per cent pleased that I too had accepted Margot de Souza's offer.

The airport was a mass of tourists, reps, taxi drivers calling for rides. We bypassed it all, whisked through security and out of the main doors, straight into big black tinted-window four-wheel drives, with our luggage travelling separately. Coco, Verity, Emmeline and Rollo got in the first car; me, Malaika and Yannis got in the second. Just as we were pulling away, the door swung open and Laurent jumped in, like a low-budget James Bond.

'Christ, you nearly left without me,' he said.

Yannis frowned. 'What were you doing?'

'Nothing,' Laurent said with a grin.

On the pavement, the blonde flight attendant from our plane was giving him an exuberant wave.

Malaika rolled her eyes. 'My god, what do they see in you?'

Laurent made a noise like the question was very unfair. 'Come on, Malaika. We can't be like this all holiday. Can't we just be friends?'

'I don't want to be your friend,' Malaika scoffed. Yannis guffawed.

Laurent held his hands up. 'Everyone, please note that I tried,' he stated, like the injured party, and then put on his headphones.

I stared out of the window. I'd never really been anywhere, even in the UK. I'd spent most of my summers on Mulberry

Island with all my friends, where we swung off rope swings far out into the gleaming river water. We lay on our backs under the mulberry trees, popping deep red fruits into our mouths, looking up through the canopy of leaves and gnarled branches at the drifting white clouds. We played basketball in the evenings when the heat of the sun had cooled, swatting mosquitos off our arms. And every night there was a barbecue or a band or a party on the old wasteland. There were young people and old people, and people who loved to dance and people who loved to sing, and people who just loved to sit while the fireflies buzzed and the fairy lights twinkled, telling stories that might or might not be true. There were huge, crackling bonfires and inky-black midnight swimming and soft hands held tight. Why would we go anywhere else, when we had all that?

But looking out at the dusty tracks of Lefkada, the eucalyptus trees, the bright blue lapping sea, I knew that there was so much out there I hadn't seen. I had felt it in New York with Ezra too – the hugeness of the world. I felt torn. I wanted all the quiet, unchanging smallness with no surprises; but then I would look out and see something like the sun-worn man in the dusty shirt standing by a van stacked high with watermelons, or the speedboat cutting through the glass-flat sea, and feel the pull of adventure, of the unknown.

I realised that Laurent was staring across the Jeep in my direction. I thought he was looking at me and felt my cheeks redden at the scrutiny. But then he said, 'Yannis, isn't that the same boat as your dad's just bought?'

Embarrassed, I looked at the sleek boat again.

'Same model. Smaller engine,' said Yannis. 'Ours is double that.'

Laurent grinned. 'Your whole island's probably double the size of Lefkada.'

Yannis laughed. He was a member of the Greek royal family. As I watched the speedboat disappear behind the seafront buildings, I felt momentarily embarrassed for thinking this was a big adventure. These people owned their own islands. This was nothing to them.

The Jeep in front indicated right and turned down a narrow side road fringed with sun-bleached pampas grass. Our car followed. I doubted Coco was even looking out of the window.

The cars wound down the narrow road, past a square with kids kicking a football and out on to a sea-trimmed dirt track. Along the roadside was a string of little tavernas. The cars kept on the bumpy track, snaking alongside the lapping water, until we reached the end of the peninsula, where they stopped. A big metal gate in front of us started to slowly open. I nudged Malaika to wake up. She did a big snore which made us all laugh, but then I was distracted by the view that opened up as the gate disappeared and the cars moved forward.

The villa was a sprawl of low white boxes with billowing

white curtains and curved terracotta roof tiles. Through the giant windows I could see a pool with white sun loungers all spaced out to face the azure sea. Waiting at the huge front porch was a man dressed in black trousers and a white jacket, holding a tray of drinks, ready to welcome us in.

'Not bad,' Yannis deigned.

I was awestruck. It was like somewhere I had seen on the TV, multiplied by a million. It was like where famous people lived. Then I realised Margot de Souza *was* famous people.

Our car pulled up by a giant palm tree. The trunk was so huge, my arms wouldn't have met round the circumference. The driver got out to open the doors for us.

Laurent stepped out, pulling on his sunglasses and chewing a stick of gum. 'Well, this is nice,' he said with a grin, tipping his head back to soak up the sun. Even Malaika had to smile.

We followed the others up the tiled path, taking a fruit cocktail from the tray.

'Thank you,' I said, then said it again in the minimal Greek I'd swotted up on the plane: 'Efharisto.'

The butler smiled. 'Parakaló.'

The drink was icy cold and sweet with mango and peach. I walked through the villa in a bit of a daze. It was sleek and modern, all bare wood and sprawling house plants. The marble floor gleamed in the sunlight. Everywhere I looked, there were windows showing off the wraparound view. Through one archway was the kitchen, a chef busily preparing food. Out the back was an infinity pool, water cascading over the edge to make it look like you could swim right out into the sea.

Coco was already poised on the terrace, looking out at the sumptuous view. 'You like?' she said over her shoulder to her brother.

'It'll do,' drawled Laurent.

She raised her glass. He raised his back. Then after a quick sip of the bright sweet nectar, he put the glass down on the long table and yanked his top off over his head to reveal a set of tanned, washboard abs. Flinging the T-shirt to the ground and the phone from his pocket on to the sun lounger, he dived cool and graceful into the water, then rose to the surface with a long drawn out, 'Yes.'

Yannis, who'd been checking out the rooms, came outside stripped to the waist and joined Laurent in the pool with a giant bomb.

Coco shrieked even though she'd been barely touched by the spray. 'Yannis, you pain in the arse!' she shouted.

Verity screamed too. She'd caught the brunt of it, selfie-ing against the sky-blue sea. Her iPhone and her baggy pink T-shirt were drenched. Yannis surfaced, choking on a laugh and Verity stomped off, seething.

Malaika caught my eye with a grin.

Coco lay down on one of the loungers, stretching out her long, tanned legs, and put her earphones in. Then she closed her eyes, her hands behind her head.

Laurent flicked her with water from the pool. 'Aren't you getting in?'

She opened one eye. 'Do I look like I'm getting in?'

More cars had arrived and the Vox crew bustled in. André clapped his hands, saying, 'Does everyone have what they need? Everyone OK?' as he surveyed us all with undiluted displeasure. At which point, Ned and Emir came hurtling out through the glass doors and catapulted themselves into the pool, soaking anyone who was still fully clothed – which meant me, Malaika and the Vox people.

'For god's sake. Why do I have to work with *children*?' André snapped.

He reeled off our schedule – free time until dinner on the terrace, and to be ready for the cars at 8 a.m. sharp – and stormed off into the house.

'You ladies getting in the pool?' Laurent shouted, and I realised he was talking to me and Malaika.

'Maybe.' I wasn't sure.

Malaika shook her head. 'Not with you.'

'Oh, come on,' Yannis chimed in. 'Can't you two have a truce, just for the weekend?'

Malaika scowled at the idea. Laurent was really grinning.

'Pleeeease, Malaika,' he said, all angelic. 'Pretty please.'

I had to look down at the terracotta tiles on the floor to stop from smiling.

'Look.' Laurent pointed at me. 'She thinks you should.'

Malaika glanced at me. 'Don't encourage him.'

It occurred to me that Laurent didn't know what my name was. That wiped the smile from my face.

Malaika looked at the pool. 'It is very hot,' she conceded.

Laurent was nodding with puppy-like exuberance.

'All right. But I'm going to find my room first.'

Malaika walked into the house just as Verity returned in the tiniest silver bikini and sheer pink kaftan. 'We're in the east wing,' she said proprietorially.

'Good for you,' Malaika replied.

I smiled, following Malaika into the house, thinking how afraid I'd been of Verity and Coco when I started at Chelsea High. How much power I'd given them. I glanced back over my shoulder at Verity's clacking heels on the poolside. I wasn't afraid of them any more. I was just wary.

The white walls in the shiny marble corridors were lined with large bright abstract canvases. I peered into one of the huge, decadent bedrooms.

'Wow, have you seen this?' I gestured through the door. Malaika glanced in and nodded approval.

We could hear Rollo and Emmeline giggling in one of the rooms as we headed in the direction of what I presumed Verity would refer to as the west wing. The biggest bedroom was already littered with Ned and Emir's stuff.

'Oh my god,' I breathed at the size of the space. The two

hulking great beds, the flash remote-controlled lighting and the snazzy en-suite. There was a giant TV on the wall with a PlayStation: the clear reason they'd picked the room.

We carried on down the corridor till we reached two corner rooms at the end.

'You have that one,' suggested Malaika.

I realised when I went in that she'd given me the larger one with the view of the sea. It was such a kind gesture, but I couldn't help cringing as I remembered my awe at the other rooms. I was so obviously the outsider. The poor relation.

I lay back on the giant bed and stared up at the ceiling, listening to the whoops and splashes from the pool. These weren't my people. Being around them was exhausting. The act was so much easier at school, when it only had to last from nine till four.

My reverie was broken by a tap on the glass.

Startled, I looked up to see Laurent, dripping-wet in his dark green shorts and bronzed torso, white-toothed grin splitting his face, holding up a volleyball.

'We need more players,' he shouted through the glass, pointing at where they were putting up a net over the pool. 'Come on!'

'Er . . .' I wasn't wearing my swimsuit and my bag was wherever the luggage was. 'I don't have my stuff.' I was half glad for the excuse, but also unnerved by the shot of pleasure at being asked to join in.

That second there was a knock on the door. The white-jacketed butler appeared with my shabby rucksack: a far cry from the monogrammed luggage he'd obviously deposited in Coco and Verity's rooms.

'Would you like your bag on the bed?' he asked.

I nodded. 'Efharisto,' I said again in uncertain Greek.

He smiled again. 'Parakaló,' he said, nicely humouring my attempt.

Laurent banged on the glass again. 'Come on!'

'OK, OK,' I said, still not knowing if I wanted to play. I stood up to close the curtains so I could get changed in peace.

'Good girl.'

Laurent's face spread into the widest smile I'd seen as I went to swish the curtain closed.

CHAPTER TWELVE

Malaika knocked on my door. 'You coming?'

'I'll meet you out there,' I called back.

Through a tiny gap in the curtain I stared out at Verity and Coco by the pool – Verity sunbathing in her barely-there bikini, and Coco wiggling out of her shorts, in bikini bottoms that matched the blue and white crop top. All I had with me was an aubergine Speedo swimming costume. I didn't go on beach holidays, so I'd never felt the need for a bikini. Quite often, back on the island, I just swam in the shorts and T-shirt I had on.

Malaika stepped on to the terrace in the most stunning bronze asymmetric one-piece with a gauze panel round the waist and red Wayfarer sunglasses. She looked the most model-like of them all. Yannis wolf-whistled.

Laurent chucked the ball at her. 'Where's your friend?' he shouted as she caught it like a pro.

'*Norah*,' Malaika said, emphasising my name, 'is just coming.'

And she lobbed the ball back to him with a force and accuracy that Ms Stowe would be proud of before climbing down the metal ladder into the water.

I moved away from the gap in the curtain, took a deep breath and changed into my crappy old swimsuit. It would have to do. Tying my hair up on top of my head, I flicked open the catch on my huge, sliding-door windows and jogged out poolside, hoping to plunge into the water before anyone noticed me.

Out of the corner of my eye I saw Coco glance up and nudge Verity. They both cast a mocking sneer in my direction. I slid as fast as I could into the pool, annoyed that I was so self-conscious, that Verity and Coco could still make me feel that way.

Laurent raised his hands. 'Finally!'

It was me, Laurent and Yannis versus Malaika, Ned and Emir. The water in the pool was just higher than waist-deep, made more for sipping cocktails than any serious swimming.

I was awkward to begin with, still self-conscious, and missed a couple of easy shots. So did Emir and Yannis – but Yannis was permanently distracted by Malaika in her swimming costume. When Coco got up and padded inside with her phone and Verity curled up and went to sleep, I felt less conspicuous.

Ned lobbed the ball hard over the net.

Laurent called, 'That one's yours, Norah!' although he could clearly have intercepted it himself.

I felt myself snap into focus. I rose up out the water, suddenly uncaring about my tatty old cossie, and thwacked the ball so it dropped, almost skimming the net. It went just far enough out of Emir's reach that when he went for it, he landed face first in the water.

'Ha!' shouted Laurent, reaching up for a high-five. 'Nice one!'

It reminded me of the basketball I'd played on Mulberry Island. All of us together, kicking about after school. No pressure to be on a team, just fun. This was the kind of sport I enjoyed the most – when it didn't matter who you were, or where you came from, or even whether you were friends.

It pained me to admit it, but Laurent played amazingly. His focus was unmatched, but he'd pepper it with humour so it wasn't too serious. And there was no shortage of praise.

'Excellent work, team,' he'd shout for every point we won, genuine pleasure on his face. And if a shot went wrong, he'd say something calmly inspiring, while Ned and Emir gloated on the other side of the net. I could see why he was captain of the polo team. He had a way of making you feel good.

We played for ages. Verity snoozed on her lounger, covered in a sheen of sunbathing sweat. Rollo and Emmeline appeared through the main doors, hair ruffled, smiles like they were drugged, and sat with their feet in the water watching the game.

'Last point,' Ned shouted.

The game was tied, and the fight for the winning point had

Rollo and Emmeline cheering us on as we splashed about with desperate, laughing shouts – until finally Laurent smashed it straight past Ned and we won.

'Woo-hoo!' Laurent shouted, punching the air and pulling us together in a hug.

I was laughing, hair wet, high on our frivolous victory. But when I felt Laurent's arms squeeze me tight, I thought suddenly of Ezra and felt weirdly guilty for enjoying myself.

Then the moment was over. Rollo scooped the ball out the far end of the pool and chucked it hard at Yannis so it smashed off the side of his head. Yannis swore, hauled himself out of the water and ran after Rollo, who was already whooping and shouting around the villa complex.

Coco sauntered back out, ending a phone call with 'Ciao, ciao', glancing around disdainfully at the noise. The glinting blue water settled. Ned did a handstand. Laurent got out, arms braced on the side of the pool, water pouring off the muscles of his back. Still smiling and catching his breath, he dried himself off with one of the plush white towels, shaking the water from his hair like a dog.

Malaika swam a couple of lengths. From the sky, swallows swooped to drink from the surface of the water. I lay on my back, floating, staring up at the sun, the endorphins of winning relaxing me, making me smile.

At the far end of the pool, by a towering eucalyptus, the

cook was lighting a barbecue built into the white wall that encircled the pool area. All around, the sound of cicadas fizzed and crackled like the fire.

Then I heard Coco's voice say, 'Norah.'

I jerked up at the unfamiliar sound of my name on her lips, swiping my wet hair back from my face. 'Yeah?'

She was looking straight at me. 'Ezra sends his love,' she purred.

I saw Verity sit up and take notice, her attention piqued by the scent of cruelty.

The corners of Coco's mouth curled up ever so gently. Emmeline glanced over from where she was cocooned in Rollo's arms. Malaika stopped swimming and paused by the edge of the pool.

Trust him, I heard my mum's voice say. Water dripped from my eyelashes. I could hear my heart in my ears like the unceasing drone of the cicadas.

'Does he?' I said. 'That's nice.'

'I thought so too.'

Coco grinned and snuggled smugly down into the fluffy towel on her lounger. I had no idea if she'd been talking to Ezra, or was making it up to upset me. Either way, it had worked. I wanted to be anywhere but there.

Verity had her hands wrapped round her knees, watching with delight as I climbed out of the pool, refusing to look at any of them.

86

Laurent paused. 'Are you the one going out with Ezra?' he asked.

I nodded, reaching for a towel.

'You're *that* Norah,' he said. And I saw the change in him, as if his brain was recalibrating. 'Ezra's Norah.'

His eyes became suddenly lascivious, the upturn of his lips wolfish. Like, in that instant, his interest in me elevated purely because someone else was interested.

Someone like Ezra.

I wrapped the towel round me and walked away back to my room. They were all as bad as each other.

CHAPTER THIRTEEN

I got up with the morning sun, earlier than anyone else, craving the normality of being by myself. Creeping as quietly as I could out of the villa, I went for a jog along the seafront, where the air smelt fresh with salt and the sweetness of sap and pine drifting in from the forest.

A few of the cafés were just opening up. One of the owners arrived in an old red 1960s Mercedes, exactly like the one Dad always coveted. I slowed to admire it, to remember when we had taken two trains and a bus to go and look at one that was for sale, that he was certain he would buy with the money from the film deal – that same money that now saw him locked up.

I jogged away from the shiny car, focusing instead on the great strips of eucalyptus bark curled on the scrubby path like crocodiles and the huge trees towering above me, their leaves flickering and flecking the ground like a blanket of sequinned sunshine. To my left, the sea rolled in gentle waves, and blue and white fishing boats bobbed on moorings next to gleaming catamarans. The path forked, one side turning away from the sea and heading down towards the town. I paused to have a drink of water and admired the view, the butterflies, the little lizards darting between rocks.

I thought about my phone call with Ezra the night before. I hadn't mentioned anything about Coco. I refused to let her get under my skin, and Ezra didn't need any more hassle in his life. The meeting with the consultant hadn't gone well and his parents were arguing about what to do next.

'It's awful here,' he'd said.

I'd sighed, wishing myself back to New York. Back to lying on the freshly mown grass of Central Park, to feel his arm tight around me and the warm, intoxicating smell of him.

'How's it going over there?' Ezra asked.

'Yeah, good.' I pulled at the tufts of wool on one of the cushions.

'Who's there?' he asked, sitting back in the chair in his room. He was trying to be casual, but I could tell he was feeling left out.

'Didn't I tell you? Malaika. Yannis and Ned. Freddie wasn't allowed to come so Laurent Summers is here instead. Can you believe it? Another member of the Summers family.'

I'd laughed but Ezra hadn't. Instead he'd narrowed his eyes and said, 'You be careful of Laurent.'

I frowned, remembering the laughing victory hug in the pool. 'Why?'

'Just –' Ezra seemed to catch himself before saying, 'He's really competitive. Likes a challenge, that's all. And

89

me and him . . . well, we haven't always seen eye to eye. So you'd be . . . you know . . .'

It was my turn to be wide-eyed and aghast. 'Ezra, are you *jealous*?'

'No!'

But I knew he was. I was suddenly so glad I hadn't said anything about Coco. Now we had both shown our weakness, our petty insecurities, and it made me love him even more.

The sun was warming up. After a drink, I set off again at a fairly easy pace along the beachside until I heard the sound of pounding feet on the path behind me.

'No wonder the netball team's so crap if that's the best you can do.'

Laurent laughed as he sped past me, then turned backwards so I could get the full force of his grin. His hair was slicked back and he'd pulled his headphones off round his neck. As he slowed, he lifted his T-shirt and swiped the sweat from his brow. I refused to allow my eyes to dart to his honeycomb abs.

'I'm just jogging,' I said, trying to ignore him.

'It's never *just* anything. That's why we win and you don't,' he said, still running backwards so he was facing me. 'We train harder.'

'You don't train harder. I've seen you.'

He laughed. This was what he wanted. 'I've seen you lot, more like, prancing about in your little skirts.'

'You are unbelievable,' I said.

90

He grinned again, falling into step beside me. 'I know. Fun, though.'

We jogged side by side for a while, big tufts of pampas grass on our right, little shops and holiday villas on our left. A couple of mopeds sped past us. I kept hoping he was going to go on ahead.

'So you're the one with the dad in prison,' Laurent said.

The frankness of the statement caught me off guard. 'Yes,' I said, because I couldn't think of any way to dodge an answer.

'I'm assuming he didn't kill anyone.'

'No!' I replied, indignant. 'He didn't kill anyone.'

Laurent smirked. 'Good to know.'

I glanced briefly to the side to see his amused profile. 'You don't have to jog with me,' I said.

'I know,' he replied.

'If it's too slow for you, you should go ahead.'

Laurent shook his head. 'No, no, this is great,' he said. 'My perfect pace.'

'I thought you just said that this speed was why the netball team were so bad?'

'I would never say anything like that.'

I stopped. 'You just did!'

Laurent made a face like I was crazy to even suggest it.

'Please go away,' I said, starting up again.

He laughed. 'I'm not doing anything. I'm just jogging.'

We carried on in silence. I tried to ignore him, concentrating really hard instead on the road ahead as it looped round and we hit the curve of the peninsula again. There were kite surfers out in the distance now, and the open water lapped at the shore.

Laurent checked his Apple watch. 'That'll do, Pig,' he said.

'Are you calling *me* Pig?' Was this some hideous insult he and Coco had thought up?

'From *Babe*,' he said, as if it were obvious. 'The film.'

I found myself laughing from relief and slight shame at my paranoia. '*Babe*? I can't believe you're quoting *Babe*.'

He looked at me, deadpan. 'It's one of my top five films. Possibly even top three.'

'*Babe* is one of your top three films?' It was my turn to be disparaging.

He raised a brow. 'You think yours are better?'

'Without a doubt,' I said as we started to jog back to the villa. 'There's a million films better than *Babe*. What about the classics? *Brief Encounter*. Or *The Godfather*. Or . . .' There were so many, I could hardly list them.

'I think you're being a bit harsh on *Babe*,' he said, faux wounded.

I was about to reply, but then I tripped and stumbled on a tree root sticking up across the dirt path. With lightning reflexes, Laurent caught my arm.

The touch of his hand was like a jolt. As soon as I was steady I found myself pulling away, my mind turning to Ezra and his warning.

'Thanks,' I mumbled, knowing I was blushing. Laurent's eyes danced with amusement.

We jogged on for a bit in silence. I was annoyed at my red-faced awkwardness. Up ahead, the tip of the villa was just visible through the trees. The old red 1960s Mercedes was still parked at the side of the road.

'Whoa, nice car!' Laurent paused, distracted by the sleek lines and gleaming paintwork. He went round the front of the car to inspect it, and then carried on round the side to look in at the cream leatherwork and admire the vintage dashboard.

It was my moment to get the hell out of there.

'See you back at the place,' I called, and took off at a sprint.

'Hey, hey, hey!' he shouted back, momentarily confused by the fact he'd been abandoned.

But I didn't stop. The villa was maybe two hundred metres away. And I was good at sprinting.

'Like that is it?' I heard him call. I could hear his feet pounding on the sandy gravel. 'You think you can beat me?'

I shouldn't have allowed myself to be goaded, but there was something about his innate smugness, his grating god-given confidence, that made me push myself faster. My lungs were starting to burn.

He was gaining. I could hear his breathing behind me.

I picked up my pace till I could hear the blood pounding in my ears, till I couldn't physically go any faster. I could feel him getting closer and closer. He was taller and stronger than me, if not necessarily fitter – but I held on in there, the terrier to his greyhound. I held on when every single part of my body was pleading with me to stop. It was a matter of principle.

Laurent reached the villa wall two seconds before me. Enough time to lean against the giant stones and grin at his success. To feign ease.

'Nice try,' he said, but he was panting.

I had to catch my breath, calm my heart down. I made the mistake of wiping my face with my vest and Laurent's eyes fixed on my exposed skin.

I turned away deliberately from his gaze, pacing for a bit while my breathing slowed. When I turned back, Laurent was gone, strolling away across the landscaped garden towards the patio doors of his room, headphones back on. Ready for the next thing, the next entertainment. He slid the glass door open and stepped inside. Not looking back.

Like the whole moment had never happened.

Coco appeared in the doorway, all casually mussed in her temple trousers and off-the-shoulder, day-glow embroidered top.

'Where have you been, for god's sake? We're leaving in five. You'd better not make us late!' Taking in my sweat-soaked clothes, she added with distaste, 'And you'd better hope your face doesn't stay that red, Norah, or you're not going to be in any advert with me.'

I didn't bother replying. Instead I went to shower and

change in record time.

Despite my hurry, I was one of the last outside, hair damp, cheeks still flushed. Laurent, in contrast, was sitting on the wall with Yannis, playing Nintendo, cool as anything. André peered at me over the rim of his horn-rimmed sunglasses and tutted. Coco snarled something under her breath.

The cars sped us away into the forest, the blue of the sea and the sky appearing in snatches through the lines of trees. After about ten minutes, we reached a clearing. There was a collective pause, everyone's eyes widening in awe.

The theme for the Midsummer perfume was A Midsummer Night's Dream. There were designers up ladders adding the finishing touches to the set, hanging lanterns from the trees and smoothing drapes of cloth. Three of the trees had been completely wrapped in white muslin, with strips of lace, pearls and shimmering crystals dripping from the branches. Fairy lights twined and looped in abundance. There was a picnic laid out on sumptuous bright velvets and silks on the dusty, leaf-strewn earth, with bowls of tumbling fruit and glass jugs of lemonade. The whole scene was set against the backdrop of the white sand beach, the sea glinting with majesty.

Next to the clearing was a crumbling old hotel, which had been commandeered as the photoshoot hub. One room was for hair and make-up, another had costumes, and the bare-floored, dark-beamed dining room was crammed with nice food for us to eat. I caught a glimpse of Margot de Souza, with her bright red hair, in the overgrown back garden, in deep discussion with a man with a curled moustache. A table was strewn with clipboards, and a small team was preparing cameras and sound equipment.

André chivvied us inside. There was no air-conditioning, but giant fans whirred in every sticky room.

'Hair and make-up!' he shouted, waving his hands like he was herding cattle.

We spent the morning being transformed into the ethereal beings required for a Midsummer Night's Dream. The standing fans whirred, rustling all the papers on the desks, and the heat rose to almost unbearable levels while Zed the hairdresser vigorously blow-dried and backcombed my hair. When he turned me towards the mirror and I saw the perfect dishevel he'd achieved, I almost gasped.

André came over and gave my hair a prod. 'Yes, good,' he said with his trademark disinterest, while I could barely tear my eyes from my reflection.

A busty woman with pin-curled hair named Ruby did my make-up and called me 'sweetheart' all the time. I kind of recognised her, and asked if she'd been to our stand at Portobello market, which made her stop and say, 'Shut up, that wasn't your stall? I LOVED that stall. It's not there any more. Where did it go?'

'We weren't making enough money,' I said.

She made a sad face as she carried on with my lips. 'Well,

I loved it, sweetheart,' she said. 'And I miss it.'

'So do I,' I replied, thinking about my mum at home working on boring white shirts all day. I wondered if she missed the stall. She never said she did. But then, I never said it to her either.

'Ladies, very nice!' Laurent was standing in the doorway, surveying the room. His makeover was finished and he was clearly bored. His face had been given a chalky-white sheen which carried over on to his torso, bare except for a woven sash of leaves, and he was dressed in cream breeches with a battered leather belt, his hair fashioned into two little points.

Coco spun to look at him. 'Are you the devil?'

Laurent turned to admire himself in the full-length mirror. 'I'm a faun.'

Coco laughed. 'You look ridiculous.'

'Thanks,' Laurent replied like she'd bestowed a compliment. Giving her a dubious once up and down, he said, 'What are you meant to be?'

'*Je suis une* fairy queen,' cooed Coco, twirling in her ripped white organza gown. Her hair was parted down the centre and pulled loosely back to show off a crown of tiny white flowers. Her eyes had been elaborately painted with greens and blues and silver under the lashes. Her cheeks were like two rosy red apples.

Laurent laughed. 'You look like a psycho bride.'

Coco threw him her fakest smile. 'I don't care what

97

you think.'

He tilted his head ever so slightly. 'Oh, I think you do.'

I wondered what it was like at their house, these two sibling snakes in a near constant battle of one-upmanship.

Coco stalked off to get some water. The rest of the boys appeared, dressed in similar attire to Laurent, except Ned, who was in a less flattering bright blanket sarong, which made Laurent burst out laughing.

'Dude, that is bad!'

Ned gave him the finger.

Verity stood up, assessing the time to be right for compliments. The boys obliged, whistling appreciatively as she flicked her long black lace-twined plait over her shoulder. She did look sensational. Her dress was made of a see-through gauze textured with delicate green leaves, embroidered with lines like bark, and glinting with diamante to make her look like some sort of magical tree. It was the softest I'd ever seen her look.

Next to me, Malaika didn't even glance up. She was deep in conversation with her make-up artist about how to achieve her look. She wasn't interested in compliments – she knew how good she looked. She was swathed in scraps of figure-hugging powder-blue lace with tiny turquoise fairy wings at her shoulders. Her curls were decorated with silver leaves and around her eyes a million tiny stick-on diamantes shone like stars.

Not to be outdone by Verity (and clearly put out that Rollo

had joined in the whistling), Emmeline stood up to reveal her own dark, smoky makeover, with bone structure to die for and wide elfin eyes that had been made even bigger with shimmering greys and blacks. Her lips were crimson and her dress was a short red puffball, like a tutu.

'I think I'm the naughty fairy,' she said with a glint in her eye.

Rollo looked ecstatic as he stepped forward and scooped her up. Emmeline giggled with delight. He did seem to make her happier, I thought, watching them in the mirror as Ruby finished my mascara. It was just a shame that in her happiness, she seemed to have lost herself.

Rollo was wearing a tartan kilt and a T-shirt splodged with dirt so it looked like he'd been rolling in mud.

'You got anything on under that kilt, Rollo?' Emir asked, pulling at the fabric while Rollo tried to dodge him and keep Emmeline aloft.

'Stop it! You'll ruin the costumes!' André shouted. 'Put her down!'

I stood up then, when I knew no one was watching. But as I moved, I noticed Laurent's gaze flick up. His eyes widened slightly when he saw my dress, black as midnight, slashed to the waist, and the skirt with its layers of sequinned tulle that pooled to the floor. I was the darkness of the forest, my fairy wings made of bejewelled stag beetles and magpie feathers, my make-up smudged like ruined mascara against the paleness of my face. But the intensity in Laurent's brief glance was enough to make my cheeks flush pink, completely ruining the ghostly effect.

'OK, OK, we need to get going,' André shouted, glancing at his iPad. 'You're all in pairs. Coco and Emir. Emmeline and Laurent. Ned and Verity. Yannis and Malaika. Norah and Rollo.'

'I want to be with Rollo!' Emmeline whined, the two of them clutching hands, inseparable.

'Why must I deal with love-struck teenagers!' André sighed, exasperated. 'You be with Rollo then, just get moving.' He jabbed at the iPad. 'Norah and Laurent, you're together. Now come on. We're wasting time.'

The way he said it made me and Laurent sound like lovers too. Laurent grinned at me. Again, I felt myself turn crimson.

'Outside, everyone!' André ordered, ushering us into the silk and lace-strung forest.

Laurent put his hand on my back. 'This way, *darling*,' he quipped.

I swiped his hand away and stalked ahead. He laughed.

CHAPTER FOURTEEN

The day got hotter and hotter. Our make-up started to run. Sweat trickled between my shoulder blades. Laurent was glistening.

'Jesus Christ,' he muttered. 'What is wrong with her?'

I was lying across Laurent's thighs, my head propped up on my elbow, trying not to be at all fazed by our proximity. I hadn't been that close to many boys. I tried not to be distracted by the scent of him, so different to Ezra: the mix of Ambre Solaire, some light zingy aftershave and the new-clothes smell of his trousers.

We were all waiting for Coco, who for the last hour had been sitting on a swing, pulling the petals off a giant flower in an attempt to discern whether Emir, who was casually leaning against a lace-wrapped tree, was in love with her or not.

The others were dotted about the forest scene in various different poses. Yannis and Malaika were dancing as best they could to no music. Ned was feeding Verity plump grapes. Rollo was meant to twirl Emmeline around when they called, 'Action!', and even he looked like his arms were starting to tire.

'Cut!' shouted the twirly-moustached director. 'It's still not right!'

'Coco, honey, what do you think the problem might be?' Margot de Souza swept on to the set as the make-up people flitted around trying to blot away our sweat.

Coco frowned. 'I don't know. I just – I'm just not feeling it, here . . .' She pointed to her heart. 'It's really difficult because I can't work out what my character is thinking.'

Laurent snorted. I turned away so no one would see me roll my eyes.

Margot stroked Coco's arm. 'You seem a little tense.'

'I'm not tense!'

'She's as wooden as a tree,' muttered Ned.

Laurent cracked up. Even Verity sniggered.

'Laurent, stop laughing!' Coco shouted, clearly nervous and het up. 'I don't know what's going wrong. I don't think it's my fault. It's the pressure.'

With a little sob, she jumped off her swing and ran a few steps away, before posing by a tree, waiting for someone to go and comfort her. Verity and Emmeline obliged. Emir shrugged, like it didn't look that difficult to him. Margot de Souza sighed deeply, then went to coax Coco back.

'It's always a drama with Coco,' Yannis observed. 'Must be very tiring.'

Laurent stretched back like a cat. 'She can't help it that I got all the talent in the family.'

I rolled my eyes a second time.

Laurent looked up at me. 'Something you want to say?'

'Nothing,' I replied, feigning innocence.

He surveyed me. I made myself hold his gaze to prove I was undeterred. I wouldn't be belittled by another one of the Summers family.

To my surprise, it worked. Like staring down a wild animal. Because instead of retaliating, he said, 'So you like to run?'

'Yeah, I do,' I said.

He nodded. 'What's your 10K personal best?'

I laughed. 'I have no idea. I don't time myself.'

He made a face. 'How can you tell if you're getting better?'

'I can feel it, I suppose.'

He snorted incredulously.

'What's wrong with that?' I asked, just as Ruby came over to redo my lipstick.

'Don't frown,' she said, smoothing my brow. 'You'll get wrinkles.' She moved on to Laurent, powdering his face and redoing his mascara.

'How can you tell if you're better than the people on your team?' Laurent asked, talking as if nothing out of the ordinary was happening.

'I don't do it to be better than anyone else. I do it for me.'

'That sounds like fear to me,' he said, maddeningly dismissive. 'There's no point in doing something if it's not to be better than the competition.'

His argument went against everything I believed, the whole ethos I was brought up with. 'I think you're wrong. When I used to go to auditions it wasn't about being better than anyone else, but about being unforgettable. My dad would always say, if you get too caught up worrying about the person who goes before you, you'll never have the focus to achieve that.'

'Is this the same dad who's currently in jail?' Laurent quipped.

I couldn't believe I'd walked straight into that one. 'Forget it,' I said.

Yannis made a face of mock pain. 'That was below the belt, Laurent!'

Laurent immediately backtracked. 'Sorry,' he said, half grinning. 'I'm sorry.'

I found it hadn't cut as deep as I'd expected. With Yannis on my side, it was Laurent who seemed the odd one out.

Yannis came and stood next to me. 'You'll learn, Norah,' he said. 'He'll do anything to stop you winning an argument.'

'Shut up!' Laurent chucked a cushion at Yannis.

Yannis laughed. 'It's true! You're like the world expert in competitiveness. And you're a dick.'

Before Laurent could reply, Margot's drawling voice flooded the clearing. 'OK, we're back. We're trying something new. Coco's just going to swing. And Emir is going to pull the petals from the flower in a little subversion of the dynamic. Coco, you're happy with that, yes?'

Coco nodded and so we struck our poses again.

The sun climbed higher in the sky, making our newly powdered skin glisten. Coco perched on her swing, while Ruby tidied her eye make-up. Emir was given the giant flower to pluck. I was even less keen to be lolling over Laurent, especially when he clicked his fingers and pointed to his lap calling, 'Here, Norah!' like I was his pet dog, and all the other boys sniggered.

Suddenly I had a thought. 'Margot?' I said.

Margot swept my way in a flutter of feathers, her green eyes wide with anticipation. 'Yes, Norah darling?'

I swallowed. I'd never spoken to her directly before. 'Maybe some of the other dynamics could be subverted too? Just to, you know, keep us fresh.'

Margot stared at me. I thought she was about to get mad, when she said, 'Yes! Let's get the life back.'

André was there in an instant. 'Change positions, everyone. Change positions,' he ordered.

The twirly-moustached director sighed at the intervention.

I glanced down at Laurent. He had his eyes shut, not paying the slightest bit of attention. I stood over him, casting his face in shadow, clicked my fingers and said, 'Here, boy. Get up!'

He opened an eye. 'Are you talking to me?'

I nodded, trying to hide my smile.

He glanced round. Verity was now feeding Ned the grapes. Emmeline was laughing as she tried to hoist up Rollo. Malaika and Yannis were trying out new dance moves, going less tango and more *Pulp Fiction*.

'Oh, for god's sake,' Laurent groaned, heaving himself up.

I took his place on the ground, spread out my skirt and patted my lap, feeling quite smug. Laurent lay down, trying to make himself comfortable on the soft velvets, draping himself across my legs with his head propped up on his elbow.

'Happy now?' he said.

'Ecstatic.'

Margot gave the set a once-over and pronounced herself happy. The twirly-moustached director took his place again, having abandoned any pretence of authority. Someone called, 'Action!'

Completely against script, because we were meant to be stationary, Laurent repositioned himself, rolling on to his back. I could suddenly feel the weight of his head on my thighs.

'What are you doing?' I whisper-hissed.

He reached up to toy with my perfectly dishevelled locks, looking up to meet my eyes, and grinned. 'To be honest, Norah, I'm pretty ecstatic too.'

'This is awesome, I love it!' I heard Margot trill. The lens of the camera was suddenly hovering above us. 'Such chemistry!'

I felt the backs of his fingers run along my cheek. And then Laurent sat up and cupped the back of my neck with his hand and was suddenly leaning in, so close that our lips were a breath away, his eyes bright on mine, the perfection of all his features magnified by proximity. And still the camera was there, like a giant fly's eye right close to my face, forcing me to hold the pose. I felt my skin get hot and my heart thunder in my ears. The touch of his hand made the whole side of my face tingle and I thought, *please don't let Ezra see this*, and I know that thought made me flinch, ever so slightly.

Next instant, the camera moved on. Laurent let go of my face, grinning as if he'd won a game I didn't know we were playing, and flopped back on to my legs like the exhausted suitor. Out the corner of my eye I saw Coco giving us death stares from her swing. I realised part of Laurent's motives must have been to show he was the more talented sibling. But mainly it felt like he was proving a point.

Making sure I knew I was the weaker party.

CHAPTER FIFTEEN

The afternoon was spent doing more of the same. There was some cringy dancing, which I was praying they'd cut my part from. There were close-ups on our faces as we stared into the middle distance or tried to laugh on cue. Verity turned out to be worse at acting than Coco. Emmeline and Rollo were great, while Emir got told off all the time for messing about. Malaika was OK, but I could tell her heart wasn't in it.

I found myself enjoying the process. I liked seeing how the camera made people's faces change, made them self-conscious or more alive. I felt the same fascination as when I used to study famous actors for hours, copy their expressions and poses. Maybe if I could no longer be on the stage, I could be behind the camera instead.

By late afternoon everyone was tired and we headed back to the old hotel buildings. Margot and the director were huddled together, replaying some of the footage. Laurent and Emir threw a tennis ball at the wall back and forth to each other, the monotony of the sound echoing our moods.

Then, as the light began to fade, André appeared in the doorway of the old hotel and said, 'It's time for the fire.'

Everyone suddenly perked up. We all trooped out through the clearing to the beach, where a giant bonfire had been built. One of the team torched the kindling, and within seconds the whole thing was crackling and spitting like Guy Fawkes Night.

'Nice!' said Laurent, walking right up to the flames.

'Stand back, please,' André shouted. 'Health and safety.'

Laurent clearly didn't give a damn about health and safety. He took a step closer, entranced by the fire.

Coco stalked over. Placing her hand on the flat of his back, she said, 'Shall I push you?'

Laurent turned, eyes almost red in the flickering light. 'Go on, I dare you.'

The tension was broken as Yannis and Ned bounded over. Laurent laughed and Coco sauntered round the other side of fire, looking back at everyone through the flames. Verity joined her. I stayed back, watching.

The whole place had been rigged for filming, spotlights illuminating the beach and the giant trees, their branches casting eerie shadows. Cameras were dotted about everywhere to capture all the different angles.

André beckoned us all together as Margot gave a little briefing on the mood for the evening.

'As night falls on Midsummer's Eve, the mischief and the magic starts,' she said, waving her arms towards the darkening forest. 'This is the time that the veil between this world and the next is at its thinnest. All sorts of weird and wonderful creatures are about –'

'Watch out, Coco!' Laurent jibed.

The boys laughed and Coco scowled.

Margot ignored them. 'The bonfire of Midsummer's Eve is to ward off malevolent spirits, but I want *you* to be those spirits. To enjoy the mayhem. I want to see you run and leap. What is it, that game children play?' She turned to André, clicking her fingers for an answer.

'Hide-and-seek?' André offered.

'No,' Margot snapped, annoyed.

André looked panicked. 'Tag? Kiss chase?'

'Tag!' said Margot. 'That's the one. Although I am perfectly happy if you'd like to play kiss chase,' she cackled. 'I want you dancing round the fire. Wave some burning sticks –'

'Don't do that!' André shook his head as if that definitely wouldn't comply with the health and safety requirements.

Margot clapped her hands. 'The camera is rolling. Have fun, my darlings.'

Coco whooped and bashed Yannis on the shoulder, shouting, 'You're IT,' before skipping off round the fire. Yannis immediately jumped up to chase her, nearly knocking over a cameraman. Rollo hoisted Emmeline on to his shoulders. Ned grabbed a burning branch from the fire and waved it like a sparkler before hurling it back and running off in the opposite direction.

I was just watching, trying to avoid the glare of the camera lens, when I heard Laurent shout, 'Look out!'

I turned just in time to see Yannis, fingers outstretched to tag me. Before I had a chance to think, Laurent grabbed my hand and pulled me fast across the sand and into the spotlit woods, with Yannis hot on our heels. Another one of Laurent's competitive tactics, but this time I didn't mind.

Laurent ran really fast. Faster than I ever would. It felt like my arm was being yanked from its socket. Twigs snapped under my feet. I could hear Yannis's breath. Coco was laughing and calling from the trees somewhere. Laurent gripped tight, his hand hard and cool. Ned appeared in front of us, laughing almost maniacally in the flickering light.

I could see, but not properly. People and camera lenses were blurry. The flames leaped and crackled. I was out of breath but exhilarated as we kept just out of reach of Yannis, who finally changed direction when he saw an easier target in Malaika.

'Stop, stop,' I shouted. 'My lungs hurt.'

Laurent pulled up by the lace-wrapped tree and let go of my hand. He was panting. 'You're pretty fast,' he admitted.

The compliment rippled through me. I couldn't reply because I had no breath left.

Out of nowhere, Malaika tapped Laurent on the shoulder and said, 'You're IT!'

'Damn you!' he shouted, laughing, and I realised suddenly that he was coming for me.

'No!' I yelped, having to set off again, this time with him in pursuit.

I glimpsed Coco watching. Malaika swept past and grabbed my hand, pulling me in the opposite direction. Verity willingly became Laurent's target, pausing coquettishly, conveniently close to a camera, to catch her breath. I glanced back to see Yannis swoop in and hoist Verity up on his shoulders to save her from being caught – but then he dropped her in a heap and Laurent reached down to effortlessly tag them both.

Margot was watching from behind the fire with the director, her face euphoric. Even André looked like he might be smiling.

I realised I was having fun. Next to me, so was Malaika.

The scene was evolving now. Laurent suddenly sprinting away from Yannis. Verity trying to sort out her dress. Coco skipping and prancing, hoping to be caught. Ned, bored with the chasing, climbing the lace tree, Emir giving him a leg-up. Rollo and Emmeline practising kiss chase. Yannis wrestling Laurent to the ground, shouting, 'You're IT! I win!' Laurent shoving him off, Yannis rolling to the floor laughing. Malaika cartwheeling for the camera; Yannis one-upping Malaika with a backflip. And on it went.

I sat on Coco's swing and Emir gave me a push. Up and down, higher and higher. I could feel my smile. I could feel the fun and the mayhem Margot had asked for. I didn't even mind the cameras watching. As I swung up and down, I realised how alien the feeling was, of letting go and letting happiness in.

Finally, the energy dropped and everything ground to a halt. André came out with hot chocolate in mismatched teacups, and light gauzy blankets that we could drape round our shoulders, although it was still muggy and warm in the darkness. The diminishing fire still radiated heat, and we sat round it in our melting make-up and now raggedy costumes. Emir found a guitar and strummed away at it pretty badly until Laurent made him stop.

'I want this to be like the end of the shoot. You off-camera. The real you, the natural you. Yes?' Margot's smile dazzled in the firelight as she nudged camera people into position to catch our supposed normality. 'Imagine someone's shouted, "That's a wrap!"'

Yannis shouted, 'That's a wrap!' and everyone laughed.

We sat in a circle on the sand.

'Anyone got any ghost stories?' Ned asked, stoking the fire. 'Any juicy gossip?'

Emmeline said, 'I've got a good ghost story.' She put her hot chocolate down.

Verity perked up. 'I love a ghost story!'

Rollo said, 'It's all bullshit.'

'It's OK to admit you're scared, Rolly,' quipped Laurent. He leaned back against the fallen tree trunk, stretching his arms above his head in a smug yawn as Rollo swore at him. Then he let his arm drape casually over Malaika's shoulder

113

next to him and whispered something in her ear.

I felt an unexpected pang of jealousy. Immediately I sat up straighter, forcing the feeling away, incredulous. How could I be jealous?

And when Malaika rolled her head Laurent's way and replied, 'We aren't friends, Laurent. We never will be. Kindly remove your arm,' I hated even more the low wave of relief that rolled through me.

I didn't want to be thinking about someone like Laurent. I tried to focus on Emmeline and her ghost story, but I'd missed the main bit and couldn't pick it up. I thought about how much I had been laughing earlier and suddenly felt disloyal. There was Ezra, alone and mixed up in New York. I thought about my dad in his cell. Wondered when he had last laughed.

As Emmeline came to the end of her story, there was a sudden, 'BOO!' from behind us that made Rollo scream and jump to his feet. Ned had crept round while Emmeline was in full swing and was now on the floor in hysterics. Chaos broke out while Rollo tried to save face by pummelling Ned hard in the ribs.

In the end, Coco broke it up by leaning into the circle and saying softly, 'I've got some juicy gossip.'

It worked. Rollo immediately stopped hitting Ned and they reformed the circle. Verity frowned, upset that she didn't already know the gossip. Laurent sighed. Coco flicked her hair and licked her glossy, plump lips. The fire crackled and spat like the flames were jumping higher to hear.

Rollo rubbed his hands together. 'Don't keep us in suspense.'

Coco preened and drew a distracting line in the sand with her fingertip. 'Well,' she said, drawing out the word, biting down on her impish smile – Margot would be lapping up her facial expressions – then paused. 'No. I shouldn't.'

Laurent yawned.

'Yes you should!' Verity insisted. Yannis and Rollo nodded in fervent agreement.

Coco giggled. 'OK. When I was in New York. Me and Ezra –' She took a breath, suddenly got all coy. 'We, you know . . .'

I swung to face her. She was grinning like a naughty child, not even glancing at me, as if this news was only for the rest of the group.

Malaika cut in. 'As in *Norah's* Ezra?'

'He doesn't *belong* to Norah,' snapped Verity.

I could sense people turning to look at me. Emmeline, Yannis, maybe Laurent. Shock had frozen my expression into place. The insidious cameras rolled.

'What do you mean?' said Rollo.

'What do you think I mean, Rollo?' Coco said with sly enjoyment. 'Let's just say it was nice to wake up next to him again. Like old times.'

It was so Coco. Never explicit, just enough to tantalize. I felt like the earth beneath me had disappeared. Like

I was tumbling down into a maze of Margot's Midsummer madness.

Malaika stood up, brushing the sand off her dress. 'That is a crappy thing to say, Coco.'

Coco shrugged it off. 'I'm only telling the truth.' She looked at me, all big, sad, mocking eyes. 'Soz, Norah.'

I thought about Ezra saying he loved me. I thought about my mum telling me to trust him. I looked at Coco. Her face flushed with excitement. Eyes almost wild.

'You're lying,' I said.

Her face hardened. 'No I'm not.'

I tried to keep my breathing steady. I knew what Coco was like. I would not rise to it this time. *Trust him.* Over the other side of the circle, Laurent was watching me with interest.

'Well,' I said, standing up. 'I don't believe you.'

'D'you know,' Laurent mused, 'I don't believe you either.'

I glanced his way, surprised by the interjection. But he wasn't looking at me. His gaze was fixed on his sister.

'What's it got to do with *you*?' Coco spat.

Laurent shrugged.

For me to deny it meant nothing. For Laurent to discredit it meant everything. Around the circle, the thrilling glow of the news faded. What had seemed unquestionably the truth was suddenly in doubt.

Rollo shook his head. 'Not convinced. Nice try, Coco.'

Coco tried to style it out. 'Believe whatever you want,'

she said, turning to whisper with Verity. But her moment had passed.

Under different circumstances I might have looked at Laurent and mouthed a thank you. But I found I couldn't look up. I just wanted to go home.

Laurent stood up and stretched. 'I reckon we're done here,' he said, yanking off his sash of leaves. '*That's* a wrap!'

CHAPTER SiXTEEN

Back at the villa, the mood had shifted. Everyone was tired and emotionally drained, like the morning after a party. Though it was late, we all needed to wind down. André sat at the kitchen island, drinking and working, ignoring us as best he could. Moths flittered round the outdoor lights, supper for the scampering geckos. The pool glimmered like phosphorous. Coco, Verity, Rollo and Emmeline lounged by the water's edge, dipping legs occasionally, muttering low. Emir and Laurent stayed inside, glued to the PlayStation, while Yannis, Ned, Malaika and I played subdued table tennis. My heart wasn't in it. All I could think about was Coco and Ezra. I wanted to speak to him so badly, to hear him say it wasn't true. But I couldn't. I had to hold faith.

When I lost a really easy point in the table tennis, I put my bat down and said, 'I'm going to bed.'

'Do you want me to come too?' Malaika asked.

Yannis started to grin and she gave him a death stare.

I shook my head. 'No, I'm fine. Just tired.'

Malaika nodded. 'OK, well if you need anything . . .'

I was quite pleased to be able to slip away. We were leaving at ten the next morning. In my room I closed the curtains, shutting out the view of Coco and company. I kept imagining her leaning across in the New York pizza restaurant and kissing Ezra. Their mouths touching with the familiarity of old times, their lips greasy, their hands still holding slices of pizza. Coco going back to Ezra's apartment . . .

I huffed a breath of frustration and yanked the curtain a bit more. Then I flopped on the bed and got out my phone. I'd just ask him. Or tell him. And laugh.

But when I scrolled through my phone, the first thing I saw was a picture posted by Ezra of him and his brother in the hospital. Josh was in a wheelchair, grinning with the nurses, Nintendo Switch in his lap. There was a pile of junk food on the table. There were dark circles under Ezra's eyes.

I couldn't ring him now. Coco had form as a lying troublemaker. Ezra had enough on his plate. That was what relationships were about. That was when trust came into play.

'Come on, Norah,' I whispered to myself. 'Get over it.'

I got up and paced the room. I threw the few items I'd unpacked back into my bag. I did some netball stretches. I was actually quite looking forward to getting back to the normality of training. I changed into my vest and little short pyjamas, white with multicoloured stars embroidered on them that my mum had bought me from the summer craft fair on Mulberry Island. I lay on my back again and stared up at the ceiling.

There was a soft knock on the door.

My whole body tensed. 'Hello?'

'It's me,' said Malaika.

Relieved, I got up to open the door. I was glad it was her.

'You know it's bullshit, don't you?' she said outright.

I nodded. 'Yeah, I do. Thanks.'

Malaika looked at me with big, sad eyes. 'Coco's an expert at getting under people's skin. So is her brother. It's a family trait. Ezra's crazy about you.'

I made a face. 'You've never seen us together!'

She waved my comment aside. 'I've seen his Instagram. I've seen his adoring face on your FaceTime. I've seen *your* face when he rings.' She laughed and I felt myself blush. 'Seriously, just don't worry about it.'

I felt the prickle of tears threatening. 'Thank you.'

She winked at me and went to her room.

I closed the door, feeling a hundred times better. Then I walked across the wooden floor and the fluffy rug to stand by the window, drawing back the curtain slightly to look out at the sea, which was lit by underwater floodlights. Everyone had gone inside. The sea was as still as the pool. I imagined the tiny silver fish congregating in the illuminated water. Remembered the night fishing we'd do on Mulberry Island: me, Dad and his friend, Tricky. When it got too cold I'd curl up on Dad's lap and he'd stroke my hair like I was a little girl while I listened to him and Tricky reminiscing about the past, smoking cigars, and on the odd occasion pulling a giant fish from the river. The idea of such simple contentment was almost laughable now.

I was startled from my reverie by a face at the window. I screamed and stumbled backwards.

Laurent rested his hands on the glass, really laughing at the fright he'd given me.

Fear gave way to anger. I threw open the sliding doors. 'What are you doing?'

He stepped back and stood with his hand on his heart, trying not to grin. 'Sorry, sorry, I didn't realise that would work quite so well.'

'You almost gave me a heart attack!' I could still feel the adrenaline pumping through my veins.

'I know, I'm sorry. Truly I am,' he said, walking into my room without waiting to be invited.

I stepped back with a frown, suddenly hyper aware of my tiny star pyjamas. 'What are you doing here?'

Prowling round my room, he paused at the sink where my toothbrush stood in a glass. 'You don't have much stuff, do you?'

'It's packed,' I said. We both looked at my small bag. I reached for Ezra's hockey sweatshirt without looking too obvious that I was trying to cover up. 'Seriously, why are you in my room?'

'Well,' he said, leaning up against the sink. 'I felt I should probably check that you were OK after my sister's little showdown and – er – well, I figured you might not open the door if I came the normal route.' He ended with a dazzling grin, like the speech was rehearsed.

'I'm fine, thank you very much. And no, I *wouldn't* have opened the door,' I said, on edge about my near nakedness, keen to get him out of my room.

His chest looked broader with his arms behind him resting on the sink stand. 'Do I make you nervous, Norah?'

My fingers were toying with the hoodie on the bed. 'No,' I said, too quickly.

He laughed, pushing himself off the sink to continue his prowl. He paused at my bedside table, with my glasses and my book. 'This is a sweet little vignette,' he said. He thought for a second. 'Do you know, I had no idea I knew the word *vignette*. Mrs Harris would be proud.' Mrs Harris was head of English at Chelsea High.

I pulled the hoodie on.

'Cold?' he asked.

The room was warm. The whole of Greece was warm.

I shrugged. 'A bit.'

I watched him take in the logo on the hoodie. Chelsea High hockey. It was too big for me and so obviously Ezra's.

Laurent nodded at the sweatshirt. 'What did he say about Coco?'

'I haven't asked him.'

He cocked his head in surprise. 'Really?'

'I don't need to. I trust him.'

Laurent's lips turned down. He nodded with interest. 'Wow,' he said, pacing to the end of the bed, one finger trailing along the gold frame.

I crossed my arms self-consciously over my chest, my hands tucked into the overlong cuffs of the hoodie. I realised that it almost covered my shorts, giving the impression that I was standing there with no trousers on. '*You're* the one who said you didn't believe her.'

Laurent held his hands up at my tone. 'I know she's an expert liar. Don't get mad with me.'

'I'm not mad with you,' I said. 'It's just you're standing there implying that I'm wrong to trust Ezra, when you were the one who said you didn't believe it.'

'Well, to be honest, I said that more because I felt sorry for you with my sister on your back,' Laurent said. 'But yeah, totally great, good idea to trust him. What is love without trust?' He walked to the window. 'Isn't that what Shakespeare said? God,' he looked at me over his shoulder, 'Mrs Harris would be seriously impressed with me tonight.'

'I don't think Shakespeare said that.'

'Who did then?'

'You,' I replied. 'Just now.'

The corner of his mouth quirked up. 'Funny,' he said. 'Anyway. That's good that you trust Ezra. Really good. Your relationship will go far.'

I felt annoyed by his patronising tone. 'Why are you here?'

Laurent came so close that I could see the flecks of brown in his green eyes and the faint tan line of his sunglasses. He smelt of shower gel, expensive and musky. I felt my heartbeat increase. I was annoyed how his closeness affected me, that I couldn't stop myself wondering what his skin felt like. He reached forward to touch my shoulder. I pulled back.

He laughed and held up a tiny feather that had been on the arm of my hoodie. He let it float to the floor.

'I told you, I came to see if you were all right. That's all.'

He was closer now, looking down at me. I wanted to step away, but something kept me there – maybe just the feeling of being looked at like that by those eyes. Eyes that had looked at so many girls in the same way. It was a practised art, but I could suddenly understand why so many had fallen for him. Like the little fish outside, darting towards the floodlights. Like the moths bashing repeatedly against the glass.

Laurent stepped closer still. 'I just know that if someone *had* let me down in the worst way possible . . . I would maybe be feeling like I didn't want to be alone.'

His hand brushed a stray strand of hair away from my face, tucking it behind my ear. In that moment I unfroze, the cliché of the gesture bringing me back to reality.

'You are unbelievable,' I said, stepping away from him. 'Don't come in here and pretend to be nice to me when really all you want to do is . . .' I waved my hand up and down at him, 'this!'

His demeanour changed in an instant. He was suddenly all cool and detached. '*This*?'

I narrowed my eyes. 'You know.'

'Clearly not,' he said with a smirk.

I laughed at the obviousness, and understood why Malaika found him so frustrating. I walked to the door and opened it wide. 'Thanks for stopping by, Laurent. I really appreciate it.'

Laurent thought for a moment, hands now in his pockets. Then he sucked in his cheeks slightly, nodded, and strode across the room. Pausing at the door, he said softly, 'Sleep well, Norah.'

I frowned at the sweetness of his tone. Poking my head out into the corridor, I spotted Verity, her eyes wide at the sight of Laurent leaving my room.

Laurent grinned, all cocky mischief. Then he sauntered away to his own room.

'Night, Vee,' he said, as he passed Verity standing agog.

CHAPTER SEVENTEEN

The next morning everyone waited impatiently in their little groups for the late taxis. The warm Greek air was stifling as I tried to bat away the images of Ezra and Coco that had plagued me all night.

Margot de Souza came to see us off, dressed in a blue and white kaftan and pink velvet slipper shoes. She air-kissed us all – 'My darlings, you were all amazing! Amazing! Such beauties!' – while pressing little boxes of Midsummer perfume into our hands.

'Yay, now we can all smell like Coco,' said Laurent out of Margot's earshot, and Coco glowered.

I managed to avoid Coco for most of the journey home. But during a particularly bad bout of turbulence on the plane, I accidentally caught her eye. She raised an eyebrow at me, self-satisfied and knowing, like she'd been waiting for the moment all morning.

I had never been more relieved to see my mum waiting at Heathrow for me, like a vision of normality. Her blonde hair loose and wavy, she was dressed in a denim boiler suit and white trainers, a black and white hounds' tooth scarf tied at the neck, her familiar red lipstick in place.

As I got closer I saw how tired she looked, but I allowed myself to be hugged tight and my bag drawn down off my shoulder and on to hers.

'My precious girl, I've missed you,' she said into my hair. 'Did you have fun?'

I squeezed her especially tight, feeling almost on the verge of tears.

She laughed at the tightness of the hug and drew me back by the shoulders. 'You look tired.'

I could have easily said the same back to her. But I replied, 'I'm OK. And yes, it was fun. Have you spoken to Dad?'

She shook her head. 'I emailed him the picture you sent in your costume, but you know what they're like.'

I did. Nothing was quick or easy with the prison service. I'm sure lots of people thought that was the way it should be. But I still found it hard to think of my dad as a criminal.

'So glad you had fun,' my mum said. 'I spent the whole day yesterday refreshing the Vox Instagram to see you.'

We were suddenly distracted by the determined strides of a silver-haired man in an expensive suit. 'Just get it done!' he was barking at some poor minion on the other end of the phone. I immediately recognised him as Coco's father, Titus Summers. Rich and mean, from what I knew of him. 'If you still want a job tomorrow, sort it out!'

The people nearby were staring, but Titus Summers didn't

seem to notice. When he spotted Malaika's father and the opportunity for some fortuitous networking, he made a beeline for him, completely ignoring Malaika. After some polite chit-chat, he huffed, 'Where are my bloody children?'

I heard Coco's unmistakable squeal. 'Daddy! You came!' Clutching a strawberry Frappuccino, she darted over on tiptoe like a little girl, her blonde waves tumbling over one eye.

'I said I would, didn't I?' Titus snapped by way of hello. As Coco threw her arms round him, he added, 'Where's Laurent?' while absently patting her on the back. 'Don't get that strawberry muck on my suit,' he added, extricating himself.

Coco looked momentarily forlorn. I glanced up at my mum to roll my eyes at the scene and move on, but she was staring at Titus, stony-faced.

Laurent appeared, his own Frappuccino in hand.

'Jesus! What are you doing with that rubbish?' Titus snatched the drink from his son. 'Do you know what this is?' He held the cup up. 'It's sugar. What's sugar? Fat. What do muscles need with fat? Nothing. Unless you want to be fat!' He spat the word accusingly before tossing the cup in a nearby bin. 'For Christ's sake, Laurent, are you a complete moron? You're in training.'

Laurent opened his mouth to say something but Titus shook his head. 'I don't want to hear it.'

Coco stopped mid-suck on her straw, clearly hurt that no one had snatched her Frappuccino away. It was the only time I'd ever felt faintly sorry for her.

Titus wasn't finished. 'And you lied to me –' He lifted up his phone to press the screen close to Laurent's face. 'There *was* a match this weekend.'

'It was just a friendly,' Laurent said, his tone pleading.

'There's no such thing as a friendly,' growled Titus. 'Jesus, Laurent. What are you playing at?'

Laurent looked down at the floor. It was the first time I'd seen him chastened. It occurred to me that Titus hadn't even said hello to his son.

'You don't piss away your future to go bloody modelling, understand?' Titus huffed. 'Idiot!'

I heard my mum tut. Titus obviously heard it too. He looked around to see where the disapproval had come from. When he saw my mum, his eyes widened and his lips parted for a split second. Then his face shuttered again. He gave her a sharp little nod in greeting and turned back to Laurent.

I looked at my mum, whose lips were pursed in distaste. I remembered my dad mentioning Titus in the Variety Performance at our last visit.

'You know him from school, don't you?' I said.

'Barely.' Mum had moved on, the moment over. 'Come on, let's go.'

Titus was still barking orders, but now seemed more

focused on getting out of the airport. His eyes kept flicking towards my mum. Had my parents' relationship with Titus been the same as mine with Coco?

My attention wandered towards Laurent, whose head was bowed, like he'd had the air knocked out of him. I noticed too that Coco had left her Frappuccino, still full, on the edge of an airport plant pot.

Unfortunately, we all seemed to be headed in the same direction.

'Lois?' said Titus Summers in an unconvincing show of disbelief.

My mum quietly sighed. 'Hello, Titus.'

Laurent and Coco were watching, eyes narrowed.

'It really is a surprise to see you,' Titus went on, displaying a big, white-toothed smile. 'And looking really well, I might add.' Then he paused. 'Is Bill OK?'

My mum almost snorted but settled on a kind of grimace. 'He's OK. How's Lavinia?'

Even I could hear my mum's insincerity as she asked after Coco's mother, another Chelsea High alumnus.

'She's just great,' boasted Titus.

'Well, anyway,' my mum said. 'We've got to go and get the Tube now.'

Titus gave a curt nod. Then his phone rang. 'Sorry, I've got to –' he said, and stalked off, all, 'Right, right!' into the phone, gesturing for Laurent to bring the trolley.

Coco trotted to keep pace with her father, but Laurent slowed for a second.

'See ya, Norah,' he said, with a wink and a grin.

My mum frowned. 'Are you friends with him?'

I shook my head.

'Good.' She said, eyeing the departing Summers family. 'Best to steer well clear.'

CHAPTER EIGHTEEN

I had never been happier to be home. The softness of my bed, the smell of my freshly washed sheets. My mum had made me a cup of tea and Marmite on toast and was now catching up on her emails in the living room while also doing yoga on YouTube. I had my cosy socks on even though it was summer, Mum's flowered harem pants and the softest mustard-yellow T-shirt, knotted at the front to cover a nail varnish stain. Outside the giant window at the end of my bed, I could see rowers and geese with trails of fat goslings, both wobbling in the wash of one of the sightseeing ribs. On the deck of the flash Dutch barge at the end of the pier I could see our neighbour Warwick sunbathing shirtless, while his boyfriend read the paper and stroked a sleek Siamese cat. On the jetty, Maurice, a moody Frenchman who didn't approve of our scruffy boat, had set up an easel and was painting a terrible picture of Battersea Bridge. I wondered if any of them could see me as I watched.

My phone rang. Ezra. My heart leaped.

'How was it?' He looked so happy to see me. 'Saw some amazing pictures on Instagram. Made me really jealous I wasn't there. You look gorgeous.'

His hair was pushed back, his thick dark lashes framing smiling eyes. The compliment made me tingle.

'Thanks. And you look much better now, too,' I said, happy that the dark lines under his eyes had gone.

'Yeah, it's better,' he said. 'Josh is doing OK. They've done more tests and the prognosis for the op seems more positive.'

'Oh, amazing!' I felt relief flood through me. I sat back, cross-legged against the wall. I couldn't stop myself from smiling.

He leaned forward. 'I really wish I could touch you.'

I leaned forward too, so our foreheads were both resting on our screens. 'Me too, I feel like if I reached forward I could hold your hand.'

'I missed you when you were in Greece. I missed this.'

'You were in the hospital, I didn't want to bother you.'

'You never bother me. You're my escape. I need you.'

I exhaled, my breath shuddery with release. I felt suddenly like I might well up.

'What's wrong?' Ezra asked.

'Nothing.'

'Yes there is.'

I wanted to bury my head in his top. 'I just want us to lie on the bed and look out of my window together.'

He laughed. 'Well, we can do that after you say what you're not saying.'

'It's nothing. It was stupid,' I said. 'Just Coco again. I tried

133

not to let her get to me, I promise I did. We had this stupid campfire thing and she said that you two had basically spent the night together when she was in New York. And I totally know you didn't. And I completely trust you. I just . . . it hurt, you know, her saying it.'

Ezra held his hand to his forehead. 'Oh god, Norah. I'm really sorry she said that. She is unbelievable.'

'No one believed her,' I added. 'Well, they kind of did, but then Laurent said he didn't and that turned the others.'

'Laurent said that?' Ezra sounded surprised.

I certainly wasn't going to add the bit about Laurent then coming to my room. The memory of him standing close, his hand tucking my hair gently behind my ear, made me suddenly get hot with guilt. Especially when Ezra looked me straight in the eye and said, all serious, 'Thanks for trusting me, Norah.'

I stared back into his deep brown eyes, realising I trusted him more than anyone else I knew. 'Thank you for being you,' I said.

The moment I said it, I felt the tension drain out of me. I felt suddenly so tired and so relieved to be there with him. Everything in my life was made better by the fact I had him.

Ezra shut his eyes. 'This is so shit, this distance.' Then he smiled and the frown in his forehead softened and he said, 'Show me what's going on outside your window then.'

Smiling through the tears that had come after all, I held up the phone. 'Well, there's Warwick, topping up his tan . . .'

CHAPTER NINETEEN

The noise of the cicadas infused my dreams. The sound rising and rising until I was suddenly awake. Sitting up, I was surprised to find I wasn't in Greece but in my bed on the boat. My alarm was going, but outside it was still dark, on the cusp of dawn. I tried to get my bearings, wiping bleary eyes. Then I realised it wasn't my alarm but my phone, and it was five o'clock in the morning.

Had something happened to my dad? Or maybe one of my grandparents? I fumbled around to find the handset, my tired eyes wincing at the shrill noise.

'Hello?' I said, my voice thick with sleep, pushing my bird's-nest hair out of my face. Outside the sun was beginning to rise. There was a duck on the deck cleaning itself.

'Norah?' It was Ezra's voice.

I sat up, suddenly awake. 'Are you OK? What's wrong?'

He was silent. I felt the cool flutter of dread up my spine. 'Is it Josh?'

'No,' he said, then he was quiet again. Then after a second he said, 'Shit.'

'What, what's going on? Tell me.'

135

'I *was* with Coco,' he said. Then, more urgently, he added, 'But it was just one night, I swear.'

Everything around me came into sharp relief. Bright and bold and painfully clear. The patterns on my duvet, the bubbles in the glass of water by my bed, the shape of my toes, the loose thread on my pyjama bottoms. I could hear my mum in the kitchen, up and making a cup of tea, opening her laptop. She barely slept these days.

Ezra was saying, 'It was just once. Seriously, it was nothing. I never meant it to happen and I realised it was a mistake as soon as it did.'

I thought about Coco's face by the campfire. The smug certainty of her smile. It seemed crazy now to imagine she'd made it up. I thought about how happy I'd been snuggled in my bed last night.

'Say something, Norah.'

There was so much to say, but I felt too stunned to say any of it. I could feel my bottom lip start to tremble and my face crease up and I willed myself not to sob out loud.

'Why would you do it?' I whispered on a shaky breath.

'I don't know,' he said, his voice desperate. 'I really don't know, Norah.'

'Yes you do. Tell me the truth. You owe me the truth now of all times.'

Ezra was silent. I could hear my heart thumping in my ears. I wanted to be back asleep and this not to be happening.

'It was after you rang asking why I hadn't told you about meeting her,' he said at last. 'I'd had the news about Josh. I don't know what happened. I couldn't handle you being jealous, it felt like another pressure. Like I couldn't breathe.'

'So you're saying it was my fault?' I could feel the tears bubbling up, unstoppable.

'No! I don't know what I'm saying. I hate myself, Norah. That I could do this to you.' He paused for breath. I pictured him running his hands through his hair. 'And you – you are a good person. You see positives. You make people see positives. I don't know how I could do it.'

I could imagine his face as he spoke. The darkness of his eyes, the raven's wing lashes as they blinked, the tight anger of his jaw. I was glad I couldn't see it.

I couldn't believe this was happening.

'Honestly, Norah, it was nothing.'

I wiped my eyes with the heel of my hand. 'It's not nothing to me. Or Coco.'

'No,' he said, quietly. 'Please, I'm just trying to explain . . .'

And then it all just became white noise. Excuses. I drifted away, listening to my mum opening and shutting the fridge in the kitchen. I wondered if my dad was still asleep. Whether he slept well in prison. Whether the beds were hard and cold or too soft and lumpy. I wondered if his room-mate snored. If it smelt the same in the cells as it did in the visitors' hall. Probably worse. I wondered if they'd let me creep in, lock me away so I never had to walk back into school and see the victory on Coco's face.

'I have to go,' I said, cutting Ezra off in the middle of whatever he was saying.

'Norah, please –'

'I can't do this. I trusted you . . .'

I didn't know what else to say. All I could see ahead of me was greyness. School would be awful. Coco would be awful. I needed to get off the phone.

'Just concentrate on Josh,' I said at last. 'That's the only good thing you can do. He's the most important person at the moment. I can't talk to you right now.'

I hung up, putting my phone on silent. Then I sat on the bed, looking out of the window. The preening duck was gone. All the other boats had their curtains closed. The sun was inching higher in the white-blue sky.

My body seemed to be shutting down like an optical illusion, a new me falling down over the old. Just like it had when I'd heard my dad's lies exposed in the courtroom. Just like it had when he'd been sentenced. Just like it had the first time we'd visited him in jail.

There were so many layers of the new me now, I had no idea where the old me was.

CHAPTER TWENTY

I sleepwalked through school that week, aware that the news about Ezra and Coco had spread like wildfire.

Daniel caught up with me after Maths. 'So it's true?'

I said, 'Hmm,' as if I was as surprised as he was, still unable to get it to sink into my brain.

Light flooded through the mullioned windows of the old red-brick building as we walked along the maze of corridors, past big oil paintings so familiar now that they blended into the background. Daniel was headed for the Great Hall and me for the sports noticeboard. There was a home game tonight, and Ms Stowe should have put the team up by now.

At the hall doors, Daniel paused. 'Variety auditions are this afternoon,' he said, pushing his glasses up his nose as he tried to lock me in a meaningful stare.

'You can't adjust your glasses while trying to stare me out,' I said. 'It doesn't work.'

He feigned annoyance that I'd seen through his tactics. 'Please audition. It'll take your mind off things.'

I saw Ms Stowe approaching the sports noticeboard from the other direction with her bit of paper. 'I have that to take my mind off things,' I said, nodding.

A netball game did actually feel like something I could channel my energy and frustration into. For the first time, I hoped I was actually on the team rather than sitting on the bench as reserve.

Ms Stowe pinned up the list. There was my name: reserve, as usual. Malaika was down as goal shooter. It was the first time I'd had to swallow down my envy.

'Forget about them.' Daniel stood beside me, restyling his quiff in the reflection of the trophy cabinet. 'You're not even on the proper team. Come and audition. You're a shoo-in for a lead, I promise.'

I shook my head. 'Thanks, but no.'

The Chelsea High stage was not for me. It was hard to imagine myself ever having enjoyed it. The idea of being up there performing, relying on my emotions, drawing on feelings I'd experienced – pain, happiness, heartache – made me shudder. The person I'd been when I loved it seemed so naïve. Also, I needed to exist in Coco-free zones, and it was guaranteed she'd be in the Variety Performance. I'd stick with being reserve on the netball team.

It started to drizzle at about two o'clock. I watched the rain fall during English, looking determinedly in the opposite direction to Coco while Mrs Harris tried to engage us in the power of love sonnets. My phone was on silent in my bag, but I looked down and saw Ezra's name flashing. I let my eyes flick in Coco's direction, where she was examining her hair for non-existent split ends. I wondered if he had been ringing her too. She turned my way, a satisfied upturn of her lips when she caught me looking.

The rain remained a light, uncomfortable drizzle all the way through to the netball game later. The other school, Saint Mary's, arrived in a navy minibus and jogged to the courts. We'd never played them before. Their coach was an arch-enemy of Ms Stowe's from her own netball days. They were huge and mean-looking and – we realised as we watched them practise passing – incredible. Even Bettina looked daunted.

'This is a good opportunity, girls,' Ms Stowe barked, her competitiveness off the charts. 'Let's show them who we are!'

Over on the grass, the polo teams were practising. I could see Coco, Verity and Emmeline trotting about, their hair flicking like their ponies' tails under their helmets. Yannis, Freddie and Emir were messing about by the stables. I couldn't see Laurent, which wasn't a bad thing. I was dreading having to face his I-told-you-so reaction at the news about Ezra and Coco. It was galling that Laurent had been right. And it made me feel more of a fool for having been so certain that Ezra was different.

I sat on the bench in my anorak and maroon skirt, my hood pulled up against the hazy damp, the droplets like pinpricks on my skin, and watched us get trounced. Not just beaten but absolutely thrashed. We couldn't keep hold of the ball in the rain. Play barely got down our end, and when it did and Malaika tried to shoot, their goal keeper just towered over her. Between her and Bettina, it was a valiant effort even to score.

My phone vibrated in my pocket. I checked it surreptitiously.

I'll stop ringing, I promise. I just want to make it up to you, Norah. To prove that I love you. I'm sorry. Let me know when you want to talk x

I stared at it for ages. At the words: *I love you*, the screen dotted with rain. Feeling a new fury rising up within me, infusing my muscles and my mind.

How easy the words were to say.

That morning, my dad had sent the short, prison-verified email about the photo my mum had sent of the Vox shoot. *Amazing! I've shown it to everyone. I'm the proudest dad in this place! Lots and lots of love, Dad xx* His emails always sounded a bit like he was on holiday somewhere. Like a postcard without the 'Wish you were here!' bit.

I wondered why I wasn't happier, when on paper there was so much love floating about. Was it because it was all just words on a page, light as balloons? No actual sacrifice to show for it. No thought of that love when they did what they wanted.

Ms Stowe beckoned. 'Norah, you're on next.'

I stood, distracted by my thoughts, unzipping my jacket and sprinting up and down to warm up. It occurred to me that I didn't want to be *told* I was loved. I wanted it to be there in actions, visible for all to see, not in kisses and hugs but in choices and decisions. Perhaps it should be rebranded: *I will not hurt you.*

The whistle blew. It was a fast change-around. A quick drink and back in play. I took my damp bib from Anouschka and stalked out on court. I was angry. I was hurt. I wanted to be worthy of not being lied to. Of being put first. And I wanted to win.

That final quarter, I played the hardest I've ever played, on my toes, leaping, dodging, attacking, defending. Fired up and furious, I delivered the ball to Malaika and Bettina over and over. I played to destroy the images of Ezra and Coco, fingers laced over pizza. Lips touching. Skin glistening. I played to refute the fact it was somehow my fault, to avenge that injustice. I played to annihilate the fact my dad hadn't loved me enough not to be guilty. I even played to prove I deserved a damn place on the team.

I saw Ms Stowe's face as we kept scoring. She couldn't believe it. Even the rain had stopped. When the final whistle blew, we still lost – but by a lot less than we could have done.

It was only as we were shaking hands with the Amazonian St Mary's players that I saw Laurent watching. I wondered how long he'd been there as Ms Stowe gave us a post-game talk where she murmured surprised appreciation at my gameplay.

As the St Mary's players walked to their bus Laurent tipped his head, hair damp from the rain, grinning his trademark dimpled grin. 'Ladies.'

Bettina and Layla were straight over to talk to him, giggling, retying their hair.

'Great game, Norah,' called Malaika, heading off. 'I'll see you tomorrow, I've got Science club.'

'OK, cool,' I shouted back, slinging my bag over my shoulder. The adrenaline of the game was dissipating, leaving me in a strange state of melancholy elation.

I walked fast past Laurent chatting to Bettina and Layla. I didn't imagine he particularly wanted to speak to me, but guessed he wouldn't miss an opportunity to rub it in. I thought I'd got away with it, but I wasn't quick enough. He caught up to me in a couple of easy strides.

'So, Ezra did the deed,' he said.

'Get lost.' I walked quicker, looking straight ahead.

Laurent kept pace, pushing back thick blond rain-soaked hair. 'Sorry. I am actually sorry. I feel responsible. Being a man and all.'

I glanced his way. 'A boy,' I corrected.

He laughed. 'Harsh.'

Annoyingly, I laughed back. Then I slowed down, resigned to the fact we'd have to chat. It took a lot of energy to keep aloof.

'I bet you've done worse,' I said, strangely defensive of Ezra.

'Maybe,' Laurent replied, a smirk telling me that he was mentally revisiting all his many indiscretions.

We walked some more. He seemed to be thinking. Then he

144

said, with surprising sincerity, 'Ezra really is an idiot.' He was looking at me. No grin this time. 'Are you all right?'

I wasn't stupid. Everything Laurent did had an ulterior motive. His friendly concern now was no doubt to try and get one up on Ezra. He didn't do things out of the goodness of his heart. All the same, it was nice of him to ask.

'I'm fine.'

I watched his mouth split into a big, wide smile. 'Liar.'

We were heading to the changing rooms at the back of the main building. It was the shabbiest bit of the school, though still in better shape than the whole of Mulberry Island Academy. The blue doors were scuffed and the bricks had been bashed with a million hockey sticks. There was a worn old bench out the front and an out-of-order drinking fountain. Inside, the changing rooms were old-fashioned and the showers leaked. The whole area was next on the list for renovation.

I needed to get changed out of my damp and sticky skirt and top.

'Good game?' I asked. His white polo trousers were black with mud.

'All right. We won but we could have done better. You?'

I laughed grimly. 'Dreadful. The other team were amazing.'

'I thought you said it wasn't about the competition?' Laurent said. 'That winning came from being the best you could be.'

I paused. 'You're right,' I conceded.

Laurent put his hand on his heart and feigned a fit of shock. Damn it, I was smiling again. I tried to change the subject.

'How do you think you'll do at the tournament?'

He was still smiling. 'We'll win, of course.'

'So sure,' I said, a little mocking, standing outside the doors to the changing rooms.

'There's no point otherwise. People say crap like it's the taking part that counts but it's not. It's the winning. Plain and simple.'

I rolled my eyes. 'You say the stupidest things.'

Laurent laughed, clearly tickled that I wasn't hanging off his every heroic word like the rest of the world. Him smiling made me smile. I couldn't help it, it was infectious.

He eyed me, leaning with his back against the crumbling brick wall. Then he said, 'I watched that film you rate, *Brief Encounter*.'

I didn't know what surprised me more. The idea of Laurent sitting down in front of a black and white movie, or the fact he'd done it because I'd said I liked it. 'Did you enjoy it?'

He shrugged. 'Bit slow. And it's definitely not better than *Babe*.'

I rolled my eyes, pitying his lack of film appreciation. He grinned like he'd said it just to provoke that reaction.

There was a sudden silence between us, the mood shifting simply because he'd watched something I'd mentioned. He'd thought about me when I wasn't there. My own finger had hovered over the Play button of *Babe* on Netflix a couple of nights after we'd got back from Greece, but I'd scrolled on for precisely that reason.

Thankfully, Laurent's attention was caught by one of the polo grooms leading a dappled palomino pony down the far path to a waiting horsebox in the car park. His eyes immediately lit up.

'Hey, come and meet Mabel,' he said.

'Mabel?'

'My pony,' he said, already striding away. 'Come on.'

I followed him.

'All right, mate?' Laurent said to the groom, before reaching into his pocket for a packet of polo mints. He fed one to a delighted Mabel. 'Hello, darling,' Laurent cooed, face pressed close to the horse. 'You're not really allowed these, are you, but you're so lovely.' The pony nuzzled him back, all big black eyes and glistening coat.

'Norah?' He beckoned me over. 'Meet Mabel. The one true love of my life.'

The groom holding the reins grinned.

I approached, tentative. I wasn't a massive horse person. 'Hello, Mabel,' I said with a small wave.

Laurent scoffed. 'You can do better than that. Here, give her one of these and she'll love you forever.'

He handed me a polo. I went a bit closer to the horse, the polo mint in my hand.

'Hold your hand flat or she'll bite your fingers off,' Laurent advised.

I immediately jolted back. He laughed and the groom chuckled too.

'She'll be fine,' Laurent said, beckoning me back. 'She's really gentle.'

I edged forward, holding out my hand flat with the mint. Mabel's big lips snuffled it into her mouth, making me smile. I stroked her soft nose and she nuzzled closer.

'All right, Mabel,' said Laurent. 'Don't throw yourself at everyone.'

I liked the feel of her warmth against my face. The softness of her giant eyes. 'She's lovely.'

'I know,' said Laurent, a bit wistful as he came closer and gave her a quick rub on the neck. 'You're not meant to have favourites, but she's definitely mine. Aren't you?' he said to the horse, his tone gooey with affection.

'We've got to go, Laurent,' said the groom.

Laurent took a step back. 'Yeah, sorry for holding you up.'

The groom gave him a quick salute, then clicked his tongue for Mabel to follow, and they trotted off to the horsebox.

'Where's she going?' I asked.

'Just to the vet, nothing serious.' Laurent watched Mabel coaxed up the ramp. 'I do feel a bit nervous, though,' he admitted. 'I hope they drive safely.'

I watched him watching Mabel, slightly incredulous. 'You act all tough . . .'

He tore his gaze away from the horsebox, puffing out his chest in jokey machismo. 'I *am* tough!'

We started walking back to the changing rooms. I was still smiling when I saw Rollo and the cricket players heading towards us.

'Get in there, Laurent!' Rollo jeered. 'Not wasting any time, Norah!' The other cricketers smirked.

To my disappointment, Laurent laughed too. 'You know me, always the willing rebound guy,' he called back.

I felt my cheeks flame. I don't know what I was expecting. I suppose some of the softness I'd seen when we were with Mabel.

Refusing to meet my eye, Laurent kept grinning at Rollo. I stalked into the girls' changing room without a backward glance.

On the other side of the closed door, I heard them laughing.

It was all just a game.

CHAPTER TWENTY-ONE

I got changed as quickly as possible, trying to think of witty things I could have said to Rollo and Laurent. The rain had started up again. I pulled on my maroon and gold Chelsea High tracksuit bottoms and anorak and ran out to get my bike.

The sky was a thunderous grey, darkening to black on the horizon. As I cycled the back streets of Chelsea, it felt like the rain was chasing me. The further I cycled, the worse it got, morphing from annoying drizzle to all-out torrential downpour. I could barely see where I was going. I tried to wipe the water from my eyes and hit a pothole, sliding to one side and only just regaining my balance in the stream of traffic.

Shaken, I stopped for a second, only to get drenched by a bus careering through a massive kerbside puddle, the water arcing over me like a wave. Yelling after the bus, I wiped dirty puddle water off my face.

As I was furiously gesticulating, a dark green Range Rover pulled up slowly, tyres deep in the puddle. Great. This was all I needed.

The tinted back window lowered and I saw Laurent's head, squinting at me in the rain.

'Norah?' he asked, as if I was barely recognisable in the downpour.

I pushed my soaking hair out of my eyes. 'Yes,' I said, trying to scrabble together some composure. I clambered back on my bike as calmly and unfazed as I could manage with the torrents of rain cascading like a waterfall – only to realise the chain had slipped off when I'd hit the pothole. 'Shit!' I snapped, dismounting to assess the damage.

I heard the door of the Range Rover open and shut. I saw Laurent's grey tracksuit bottoms approaching, emblazoned with sponsorship logos.

'Get in the car,' he ordered. He took my bike, easily lifting it with one hand. Going round to the boot of the car, he chucked it in.

'What are you doing?' I shouted over the drumbeat of water.

'If I'd asked, you'd have said no,' he shouted back, slamming the boot shut, now soaked himself. 'Get in!'

'No, I'll make it all wet,' I shouted, standing stubbornly, eyeing the plush cream seats of the chauffeur-driven four-by-four.

'Just get in the car, Norah. You can pay for the valet if it makes you feel any better.' He swiped water out of his eyes. The car was holding up one of the lanes of traffic and a bus, stuck behind them, beeped its horn in irritation.

With no other feasible option, and the rain somehow getting even heavier, I dived into the back seat. Laurent climbed in after me. He pulled the door shut and the car cruised out into the traffic.

'Jesus,' he said, 'I'm soaked.'

I looked around the car – plush, cream and perfect – and felt like I'd been elevated into another world.

'Where to, miss?' the chauffeur asked, meeting my eye in the rear-view mirror.

'Just by Albert Bridge, please,' I said awkwardly. 'If it's not out of your way. Otherwise I can get a bus.'

'You're not getting a *bus*,' Laurent scoffed.

I wondered if he'd ever got a bus in his life.

'Albert Bridge it is,' said the driver.

I settled back in my seat, conscious of my soaking clothes and bedraggled appearance. I felt the leather underneath me start to warm up and for a moment worried I'd somehow wet myself, before realising it was a heated seat.

Next to me, Laurent leaned back, arms stretched wide like a bird with its wings spread out to dry. Out the corner of my eye, I could see his slicked-back hair, glistening skin, and the slight annoyed curl of his lip. Somehow, being soaked made him even more good-looking.

I stopped looking at him.

The driver said, 'Laurent, do you want me to drop you off first?'

'No it's OK, Wilson.'

'Just to warn you, with the traffic, you might end up being late for –'

'It's fine,' Laurent cut him off, relaxed but adamant.

'Very good.'

I wondered what it was Laurent might be late for in order to take me home. One on one, it was harder to gauge his motives.

I made the mistake of glancing over just as he was looking at me. In the confines of the plush car everything felt more visceral. It was as if suddenly we were meeting for the first time in the real world, outside the roles and hierarchies of school. He was morphing into a real person in front of my eyes.

The condensation from our damp clothes misted the glass as the car stop-started through the London traffic. I shifted further towards the door, gazing purposefully out of the window. My instinct told me that Laurent could sense my unease. I knew nothing was going to happen between us – Laurent wasn't my type and I wasn't his – but suddenly I wanted the safety barrier of Ezra back to separate us again.

When the Range Rover purred up to the jetty, I leaped out the car with an effusive, 'Thanks so much, I really appreciate the lift,' to neither Laurent nor Wilson in particular.

'No problem at all, miss. Let me just get your bike,' Wilson said.

'I'll get the bike,' said Laurent. 'And Wilson, I'll see myself home.'

'Very good,' the chauffeur replied and pulled away into the traffic.

I sighed and hauled my kitbag on to my shoulder. The weather was now brightening, and the glinting sun mocked my dishevelled appearance as we walked round to the boot. Whatever Laurent's motives, he'd saved me from being stranded in a monsoon. So as he lifted the bike on to the pavement, I finally met his eyes and said, 'Thank you.'

He grinned, like he knew the effort it had taken to say it. 'You're welcome.'

I went to get the bike off him. Laurent shook his head, starting to push the bike towards the boat. 'It's no problem and you've got your bag.'

The jetty was dark and slippery, the wet wood sparkling in the newly appearing sun. My disapproving French neighbour, Maurice, was sweeping puddles of rain off his deck. He paused when we approached.

'Afternoon,' said Laurent as we passed, his cut-glass accent and polo kit making Maurice look twice. 'Who doesn't love an English summer, eh?'

Maurice chortled, snared by the golden halo of the Summers family. 'It is the worst,' he said, his French accent thick and, for the first time in my hearing, jovial.

Laurent shrugged. '*Apres la pluie viendra le beau temps!*'

154

Maurice threw up his hands, '*Ah mais oui, mais oui!*' he laughed, delighted at Laurent's casual slip into French.

'*Blah blah blah,*' I muttered under my breath as we moved on.

'You're just jealous that your language skills aren't up to scratch.'

'No I'm not. I just don't want to be all neighbourly to the man who wants to evict us.'

Laurent raised a brow. 'He wants to evict you? Why?'

'He thinks we lower the tone.'

I wished I'd never started this chat. In the rain our boat looked particularly the worse for wear – the rust on the metal more vibrant, the wood round the windows all cracked and peeling. But it still oozed charm with its bright colours and pot plants and all the intricate fretwork.

Laurent looked from our boat to Maurice's modernist white 'floating house', all glass and chrome and architecturally designed. 'I can see why he thinks it lowers the tone.'

'You are such a snob!'

Laurent looked affronted. 'I'm not saying *I* think it lowers the tone. I can just see why *he* might think so.'

As I climbed the steps to the deck, with their peeling buttercup paint, I missed Ezra like a sudden stab in the chest and his immediate appreciation of our boat; his response to the colours, the giant windows, the views, the ornate lanterns, the very notion of living on the river, the freedom. I had enjoyed being swept up in Ezra's fantasy of boat life. I remembered lying on my bed with him, watching the snow fall gently outside the window, lulled by the bobbing waves beneath us.

Laurent cut in on my memories. 'I'm not a snob,' he protested from the jetty. He looked completely out of place, with his polo kit and perfect features, bred from the highest pedigree. I watched him taking in my mum's wind chime, the haphazard array of terracotta pots, the vintage metal box that said POST, the brightly coloured plastic Mexican bunting. I could only imagine what the Summers house looked like, but I knew that this had to be a million miles away from what he was used to.

'You're the biggest snob!' I had to laugh at his audacity.

Laurent looked like he was about to argue, then he smiled and said, 'Maybe.'

We were both silent for a moment. The shared joke. The banter. It felt almost like flirting and I was immediately hyperaware of his presence again. The quicker I could get him to leave the better.

I realised he was still holding my bike. 'Oh damn.'

'What?' Laurent asked.

'Nothing,' I said. 'It's just I never bring it home. My mum doesn't know I have it, so I hide it.'

He made a face like that was crazy. 'Why?'

'Because it was a present from my grandparents. It's too complicated to explain. Just, you know –'

'Families?'

I paused, remembering his dad's tirades at the airport. It made me feel more kindly towards Laurent. I didn't want to feel kindly towards him, though. I wanted him to go back to his plush car and drive off back into his plush life.

'Just leave the bike there, it's fine,' I said, gesturing to the railing. 'Hopefully Mum'll get in so late she won't see it. I'll move it tomorrow.'

The sky was darkening again, another storm edging closer.

'Hadn't you better go?' I said into the silence.

He seemed in no hurry to move. 'It's polite to invite a person in, you know.'

Oh god. 'But you had somewhere to be,' I said.

'Nowhere important.' He shrugged, all blasé but still with that hint of enjoyment. Life was a constant source of amusement for him. 'Now you have to invite me in,' he added, 'because it's about to rain again and I told Wilson to go.'

How had I fallen into this trap? I shook my head in despair, then unlocked the front door. He bounded down the steps after me like a Labrador, delighted to have got his own way.

Inside, I kicked off my shoes and hung up my bag in the cupboard by the door. Laurent took his off too. Then I walked down the narrow corridor, turning the lights on, flooding the space with a yellow glow. I heard the slight intake of Laurent's breath. It wasn't quite a gasp, but enough to know that the place affected him. The textures and warmth and style couldn't be discounted because of the shabby façade.

I pretended not to look as Laurent gave himself the tour, examining the rows of art and theatre books on the wall that separated the living room from the rest of the space. He glanced into the living room with its cushions and throws and plants, then stood back to take in the kitchen with its hanging pots and Spanish tiles. It was my opinion that if you didn't love this place then you had no soul. Or at least, no soul that would have anything in common with mine.

Inspection over, he leaned against the kitchen counter. 'Not a bad place.'

'I like it,' I said, deliberately playing it down. I still didn't trust Laurent, and I wouldn't have chosen to invite him into my home.

'Can I see your room?' he asked.

'No,' I said, walking round him to put the kettle on.

His laugh was annoyingly infectious. I felt myself smiling.

'Is it this way?' he said, heading off down towards the back of the boat.

I abandoned the tea I was making and jogged to follow him. 'You're not going in my bedroom.'

'Too late,' he said, eyes ablaze as he leaned on the door handle to my tiny cabin.

Momentarily, I found myself embarrassed at the size

of it. My cosy, well-loved bedspread looked suddenly threadbare. I cringed at my teddy and my star pyjamas. I imagined Laurent at home later, lounging on some designer sofa, filling Coco in on all the details of my pitiful existence. The cackles of laughter.

He bent his head slightly and stared out of the giant window that filled the entire back wall. Then he said, almost breathless, 'Bloody hell, look at that view.' He inched closer, not once putting a hand on my bed, just leaning to see better. 'That's the most incredible thing.' He glanced back at me, entranced. 'This is what you go to sleep looking at?'

He stared again. At the twinkling lights of Albert Bridge, the purpling bruise of rain edging ever closer, and the water, black like tar, alight with the glinting reflection of the bridge. His shoulders were blocking half my view, but it seemed way too intimate for me to climb on my bed to see the rest. I became more and more conscious of the fact we were in my bedroom. That the smell of him was invading the space: Laurent's presence where it had been Ezra's. I wondered what Ezra would think if he saw us now. I was losing the ability to act naturally, suddenly too aware of my breathing, of how close we were standing. Of his hand inches away from my pyjamas.

'I could stare at that all night,' he said with a sigh. He turned unexpectedly and somehow boxed me in. We were now face to face.

He grinned slowly. 'It's very cosy in here, isn't it?'

I had no idea what to do next. Luckily, I didn't have to decide because we were interrupted by a loud rapping on the door.

CHAPTER TWENTY-TWO

I was relieved to squeeze past Laurent and head down the corridor to the front door. He followed me.

Outside the new storm had nearly reached us, the sky threatening, the clouds hovering on the cusp of another bout of torrential rain. A man in a sharp cream suit turned, smiled gleaming teeth.

'Hello, Norah Whitaker! Remember me?'

I stared. I knew exactly who he was. 'Mr Blake?'

Vincent Blake – the suave prison kingpin who'd had my dad so in awe. I tried to act like it was completely normal that a man I'd met once in a prison was now standing on my doorstep. He was dressed like he'd stepped out of a Savile Row tailor, with a blue handkerchief in his top pocket and a matching cravat. He made the boat look small.

His smile stretched wider, his eyes hawk-like behind thin gold-framed glasses. 'Indeed. A free man. I'm sorry for calling in unannounced. Very rude. But I was in the area and it's about to bucket it down. Your father was always very effusive about your hospitality.'

There was something slightly off with the words, the

expression behind his eyes. He didn't look like someone who walked around much, especially not in an expensive cream suit. I wondered how he had found himself 'in the area', needing shelter from the rain. He had the look of someone with a chauffeur. Or, at least, the money for a taxi.

'May I come in?' he said.

'Of course,' I said, strangely reluctant, as if giving a vampire permission to step over the threshold.

Ducking his head, Vincent Blake walked on to our boat like he owned it. His shoulders filled the corridor.

'Very nice,' he said, surveying the interior as Laurent had done half an hour before. But unlike Laurent, it felt like Vincent Blake was stripping it bare. His shoes tapped the floor as he perused every last thing.

'The boyfriend?' he asked, clocking Laurent in his polo kit, the obvious wealth.

I felt myself flush red. 'No.'

Vincent made a face at Laurent. 'What's wrong with you, boy? Stunning girl like this?'

Laurent shrugged, a grin of easy camaraderie on his face. 'She won't have me, Sir.'

Vincent was visibly pleased by the fact Laurent had addressed him as sir. He carried on examining the room. I glanced at the clock, wondering when my mum might be home. I hoped right now.

To break the stilted silence, I said, 'Do you want a cup of tea?'

'Love one.' Vincent made himself comfortable on the sofa. 'Your dad said you'd be a treasure.'

I felt myself starting to sweat. I wanted to somehow catch Laurent's attention, to convey the weirdness of this impromptu visit. For him to acknowledge the air of foreboding in Vincent's manner, to tell me I wasn't being paranoid.

'So you're a polo man,' said Vincent to Laurent.

I made the tea as Laurent chatted happily about himself. My hands were shaking. What was Vincent Blake doing here? This man was no small-time criminal. Just seeing him in the prison told me that he was top dog, not to be messed with, simmering with power.

The whole time Laurent was talking, I sensed Vincent's eyes on me. Like a tiger on my sofa, waiting to gobble us all up.

I told myself to calm down. This was just a nice man who had been in jail, who had done his time and was now free. He just wanted a cup of tea and somewhere friendly to shelter from the rain.

I looked at the clock again. *Please let Mum come home.*

I put the tea down on the coffee table, my shaky hand spilling the liquid. 'Sorry,' I said, flustered.

'It's just tea,' said Vincent, slow and amused.

'Biscuit?' I said, slightly out of desperation. 'Ginger nut?'

'I'll have one,' Laurent piped up. 'Love a ginger nut.'

I went and got the biscuits, wondering if Vincent Blake had a gun.

Laurent was asking Vincent how he knew me.

'I know her father,' Vincent said. 'A good man. Very loyal.'

Loyal. The word stuck in my mind like a pin.

We didn't have any ginger nuts. I got out the custard creams, wanting this to be over, to hurry Vincent's tea along and get him to leave.

'You said you had ginger nuts,' Laurent whined. 'They're my favourite.'

'Well, we DON'T!' I snapped.

'Good lord,' said Vincent. 'Are you sure you aren't together? You bicker like an old married couple.'

Laurent stretched back in the chair. 'Norah's with someone else, unfortunately. Turns out he's a bit of a rat, though. Just got off with my sister.'

Vincent sucked in his breath. 'Norah, Norah, Norah. Tell me the toerag's name and I'll sort him out for you.'

Laurent grinned, 'Ezra Mont—'

I cut Laurent off. 'Forget it,' I said. 'We're not together any more.'

Laurent sat forward. 'So it's over?'

I shot him a look.

Vincent folded his arms across his chest. 'Just give me his name, Norah.'

Even Laurent looked unsettled now. Vincent chuckled, like he'd been winding us up all along. And it had worked. I was coiled like a spring.

164

'So,' said Vincent, taking a sip of his tea. 'Have you heard from your dad recently?' I couldn't tell if his voice was politely inquiring or laced with intent.

'We had an email the other day.'

He nodded. 'And where's your lovely mum? What a beauty she is,' he added for Laurent's benefit. I winced.

'At work, is she?' Vincent went on. 'A little late for her to be home, no?'

'It depends,' I said, deliberately vague. 'It's quite busy at the moment, start of the new season.'

'Does the men's shirt industry have seasons?'

His eyes were unblinking, like a lizard's. The little hairs on my arms stood on end. He knew what my mum did for a living.

Laurent ate a custard cream and made a face. 'A ginger nut is by far the superior biscuit.'

Vincent laughed. I wished he would leave.

'Well,' he said, putting his half-full cup of tea down on the coffee table. 'If I could just use your facilities, I'll be off. Perhaps you could show me, Norah?'

Something in his expression made me do as he said. We left Laurent munching his way through the biscuits and checking his phone.

Outside the rain had started to pitter patter. Where the kitchen narrowed into a corridor that led to the bedrooms and bathroom, Vincent paused.

'It's this one,' I said, pointing to the bathroom door. My

eyes flicked to the fake medieval axe mounted on the wall that my dad had stolen when he was an extra in a Beowulf TV series. I could always use it as a weapon.

Vincent saw and huffed a little laugh. 'No need to look so worried, Norah. I just wanted to have a little chat with you, in private. About your father.'

I swallowed.

Vincent smoothed the front of his shirt. 'It's nothing too serious. Just that your father owes me a little favour and – how should I put it . . .' He paused. 'He has become somewhat *reluctant* to comply.'

I stood there, suddenly terrified, my heart banging in my ears.

His eyes assessed me. 'I think you are the one to give him a little nudge, Norah.' His lips stretched over his teeth in a crocodile smile. 'You look very persuasive to me. Now this door leads to the bathroom, you say?'

I walked slowly back to Laurent. My dad owed Vincent Blake a favour. Laurent started to say something but I shushed him. He frowned. I couldn't look at him. Instead, I tidied up the mugs, busying myself.

Vincent came out into the corridor, rubbing his hands with the fig hand cream we had in the bathroom. 'This is nice,' he said, giving his hands a sniff. 'Very fragrant.'

I was finding it hard to even muster a polite smile now.

He picked up on every ounce of my discomfort. 'Give my

love to your mother,' he said. 'And be sure to let your dad know we had this chat when you are next in touch.'

Outside, the rain was pecking at the glass with more urgency. Laurent put his phone away and glanced out of the window. 'Are you sure you want to go out in this?'

I glared at him.

Vincent turned the collar of his suit jacket up. 'Bit of rain never hurt anyone. I've been in much worse. Nice to meet you, son. And a pleasure to see you again, Norah,' he said, opening up the door to the elements. 'You take care now.'

I swallowed a lump in my throat. What had my dad got himself mixed up in?

I watched Vincent go, then closed the door, leaning on it with relief and shutting my eyes. When I opened them, Laurent was watching me.

'What was all that about?' he asked.

'Nothing,' I said, going past him into the living room so I could look out of the window and check that Vincent had gone. I caught the shadow of his cream suit disappearing up the jetty.

Laurent came to stand next to me at the window, jokes forgotten. Our shoulders were touching.

'You're shaking,' he said.

'It's cold.'

'No it's not.'

I wanted my mum to come home. I needed to talk to my

dad. I didn't know if I was overreacting, that perhaps it *was* just the small favour Vincent had implied. But then suddenly I was distracted because Laurent's hand brushed mine, nothing more, and a spark shot through me. He must have felt it too, like an electric shock. He paused. He looked from his hand to me.

Outside, the rain started hammering on the water, harsh and fast like ball bearings, rattling like the roof might cave in. I could sense the closeness of him, the intoxicating smell of lemons and mud and the earthiness of horses.

Laurent slowly put his hand on my shoulder. His green, narrowed cat-like eyes were so completely different to Ezra's sad brown ones. His shoulders were broad, his muscles lithe. He had none of the sharp, distinguished angles of Ezra, none of the quiet dishevelled beauty.

A thousand things ran through my head. A helpless, surging anger that my dad was up to something and it wasn't good. A self-pitying loneliness that my mum was never home, leaving me to deal with the likes of Vincent Blake. I looked at the fleck of brown in Laurent's green gaze, the perfect dip of the cupid's bow in his top lip, the smudge of mud from the polo field on his brow. And there was a tiny, furious part of me that thought if I just leaned in a fraction, my lips would touch his, in the same way that Ezra's lips had touched Coco's. An eye for an eye. A kiss for a kiss.

I found myself tipping my face up. I couldn't believe I was doing it.

His head bent and his lips met mine, soft and electric. His hand moved to my lower back with well-practised pressure, sending shivers up my spine. I felt myself disappear for one fleeting exquisite second.

The next moment, the front door opened. I heard my mum's sharp intake of breath. We sprang apart like naughty children, my lips tingling like they'd been burnt.

'What the hell do you think you're doing?'

She was drenched, arms laden with bags of shirts and fabric samples, hair in long wet ringlets. Her eyes were wild, her cheeks flushed. 'Get out,' she snapped at Laurent.

Laurent physically jerked back. 'Mrs Whittaker, I –'

'Now!' she ordered, dumping all her bags in a pile on the floor, clearly trying to rein in a tight, coiled anger that I'd never seen before.

'What's going on?' I asked, floundering. 'You can't tell him to leave.'

Laurent looked perplexed. But charming parents was a solid part of his repertoire. With a voice like syrup, the epitome of good manners, he began, 'It's fine, Norah, I'll go. Mrs Whittaker, we were just –'

'I don't want to hear it, I just want you to leave,' said my mum, cheeks pink, not looking at either of us.

'Wait,' I said, holding Laurent back with my hand, the touch immediately weirdly familiar. Adrenaline was still thumping like a beat in my ear. 'What's going on? Why are

169

you ordering him around? Do you know who's just –'

Mum seemed to have composed herself. She had wiped the rain from her face and was back to being the adult in the room. Holding up a hand, she cut me off. 'I'm sorry,' she said. 'It caught me by surprise, Laurent, to see you here. I shouldn't have snapped.'

She gathered the shirts up and draped them on the back of one of the dining chairs. Her voice was too moderated. Void of emotion.

'I completely understand, Mrs Whittaker,' said Laurent. 'I'll go.'

My mum smiled a smile that didn't reach her eyes. The boat felt suddenly very small, the rain outside very loud.

'But it's pouring,' I said.

'I'll get a cab.'

'There won't be any cabs,' I said.

He shrugged like it didn't matter. 'I'll run home.'

My mum sighed. 'You can't run home, Laurent. Can't you call someone?'

He smiled his award-winning, dazzling white smile. 'I like nothing better than a run in the rain.' And before anyone could stop him, he grabbed his shoes, breezed past us both with a wink and was gone, into the rain-lashed darkness.

'What just happened?' I asked, completely at a loss. Everything was swirling round in my head. The feelings of kissing Laurent muddled with how much I missed Ezra.

The grin Vincent Blake had given me as he'd stalked out the door. Everything was turning the wrong way, the world in confusion.

Mum started straightening out all the work she'd brought home, getting her laptop and loads of papers out of her bag. 'Norah, I'm tired. It was just an overreaction. I'm sorry.' She kicked her shoes off and, putting her slippers on, padded over to the kitchen. 'I just don't want you getting together with someone from the Summers family.'

'I'm not getting together with him.'

'And what about Ezra?' Mum said. She flicked on the kettle. 'A minute ago we were talking about building trust, and now you're with this guy? I have to say, I'm disappointed.'

I stood dumbfounded, realising how little she knew of my life at the moment. 'You don't know what you're talking about!'

'Stop, Norah,' Mum said as she poured hot water on to a camomile tea bag. 'I'm tired and I won't be spoken to like that by my daughter when I get home.'

I watched her, listened to the flat monotone of her voice. At least when she was shouting, there was some emotion. I wanted to cry with confusion and frustration. This wasn't the way things were meant to go. I wanted to tell her about Vincent Blake. But she wouldn't look at me. Instead she took her tea and went to sit at the dining table to do her work.

As I stood there, torn between walking away and trying to

reason with her, she added, 'You're not to hang around with that Summers boy. Understand?'

The idea that she could take against Laurent when I'd just been serving English Breakfast tea to an ex con was laughable. I found myself saying, 'You can't tell me who to hang around with.'

'I can,' she replied, voice sharp.

I felt my bottom lip tremble. My body was exhausted, my brain overwhelmed. 'But *why*?'

'Because I said so,' she said, finally looking up, blue eyes burning.

In the tight confines of our boat, we had never been so distant. She'd judged me unfairly about Laurent without giving me a chance to explain, and I had been left to fend for myself too much now to bow to orders.

'It doesn't work like that any more, Mum,' I said.

I was about to stalk to my bedroom when I heard her say in soft resignation, 'There's a chance he's your brother, Norah.'

CHAPTER TWENTY-THREE

I've never pushed myself so hard at netball training. Twice I had to run out of the gym to retch in the toilet. Ms Stowe was on a mission to toughen us up, and I was perfectly happy to go along with it. Anything to deaden the confusing feelings inside me. Anything that might relieve them, just for a second.

We were doing free-weights circuits. Four rounds, thirty seconds per station. Bench press, back squats, lunges, cleans all interspersed with sprint runs, sit-ups, skipping and plank. Ms Stowe didn't believe in the benefits of interval training, saying rest and recovery periods were for wimps. All of us were dripping with sweat, and each thirty seconds was starting to feel like an hour.

The tinkle of the piano and crescendo of big band numbers from the Variety Performance auditions in the Great Hall punctuated the clashing of our weights. The sound felt like another life.

'No slacking,' Ms Stowe bellowed.

'Jesus!' Malaika gasped. I could see her tiring in front of me, her arms shaking as she tried to lift the bar above her head.

I'd have taken another half hour. I wanted the punishment.

I kept replaying the scene of last night in my head, Mum's words ringing in my ears. *There's a chance he's your brother.*

Not only had I possibly kissed my brother – well, half-brother, but that didn't make it better, and oh god, I had enjoyed it, I had wanted it to carry on – there was a chance that my dad – my stupid, frustrating, lying, loveable dad – might not be my dad. And to make it all a thousand times worse – I forced my shaking arms into another press-up – Coco, of all people, might be my half-*sister*. It was too horrible to contemplate.

As my mum had told me about the one-night stand with Titus Summers, I had listened like I was hovering, out of body. It had been a stupid mistake. It was unlikely he was my father, but she couldn't be one hundred per cent sure. And then, worst of all, her eyes plaintive: 'Your dad doesn't know. Please don't tell him.'

So I had promised. Anything to hold my precious family together.

When Ezra's name flashed on my phone later that night, I just turned my phone off and watched it slip from my hand on to the pile of clothes on the floor.

'Norah!' I heard Ms Stowe shouting. 'Norah, we've finished! Stop!'

I looked around. Everyone else was sitting slumped on the gym floor staring at me as they sucked on water bottles and towelled sweat from their faces, while I was still going up and down in my press-ups, face bright red, body wrecked.

'That was pretty crazy,' said Malaika as we got changed after our showers, standing in our pants and T-shirts. 'You were like a girl possessed.'

I laughed it off. 'I was in the zone.'

She narrowed her thick lashes. 'I was in the zone, Norah, but I could still hear Ms Stowe.'

We were pretty much alone in the changing room. Most people had gone home already. Anouschka was half dressed in the corner, on the phone to her mother, arguing. I sat down on the wooden-slatted bench that ran round the whole room and pulled on my turquoise tracksuit bottoms. Above me was a row of pegs with a few random clothes and towels left on the hooks.

Malaika sat down beside me. 'Tell me to mind my own business, but is everything OK?'

At that point, through a gap in the little windows above us, came Laurent's voice. 'Yo! Anyone in there?'

I froze.

Malaika rolled her eyes. 'Yes!' she shouted back. 'Go away.'

I heard Laurent laugh. 'Ahh, my darling Malaika, as much as I love you, I'm looking for Norah. Is she there?'

I immediately shook my head, eyes pleading for Malaika to tell him I wasn't. Malaika's eyes narrowed.

From outside Laurent said, 'Is she there or not?'

Malaika shouted in irritation, 'I'm just going to see if I can find her, hang on!' Then she looked at me, all big eyes, waiting.

'We kissed,' I hissed. 'It was a mistake. I don't want to talk to him.'

'You did what?' Malaika was so shocked, she screeched.

From outside Laurent shouted, 'What's going on? Is she there? Nooorah!' he sang like a serenade.

I closed my eyes and sighed. 'I'm here, Laurent. I'll be out in a second.'

Malaika shook her head at me. 'I can't believe you kissed Laurent.'

I didn't want to say that that was the least of my problems right now. Instead I pulled on my T-shirt, stuffed my clothes into my bag and my feet into my trainers. 'Neither can I.'

'Good luck,' Malaika called after me as I left the changing room.

Laurent jumped down from the bench he'd been standing on when he saw me. 'Were you hiding from me?'

I nodded, pulling on the backs of my trainers.

He laughed, amused by the fact that anyone would try and avoid him. 'You look like you've just got out of bed.'

I looked down at myself. My hair was wet from the shower. My once white T-shirt had been dyed a faint strawberry in the wash. And my tracksuit bottoms were threadbare. It was an outfit best described as a relaxed shambles. 'I wish I had,' I said, cloaked in a strange feeling of otherworldly calm brought about by exhaustion. 'I'm knackered.'

Laurent fell into step beside me. 'You know, I did run home last night. Bloody miles.'

I laughed without thinking.

I couldn't tell him what my mum had said.

He nudged me on the shoulder. 'That was interesting, wasn't it? Yesterday. Until your mum walked in.' He made a face. 'Is she really overprotective?'

Yannis was in the car park, getting into a huge black limo. 'Laurent, you want a lift?' he shouted, lifting up his sunglasses, intrigued by the fact we were together.

'Nah.' Laurent waved him away.

Yannis grinned. 'Enjoy!'

I frowned. 'Did you tell him?'

Laurent feigned innocence. 'Tell him what?'

'About – you know!' I couldn't say it as we walked past the car park to the side entrance of the school.

'Our *kiss*?' Laurent said, emphasising the word like it was the naughtiest in the world.

'Shush!'

He barked a laugh. 'It's OK, it is allowed: kissing.'

Ned strolled past, huge bag of polo kit slung over his shoulder. 'Who's kissing?'

'No one's kissing,' I said as he overtook us. Ned raised a disbelieving brow.

'You're only making it worse,' sighed Laurent. 'Although I'm not sure why you're so intent on hiding our love.'

'Will you *shut up*!' I hissed, stopping by my swanky bike. For once, I'd managed to snag a space in the school racks.

'So what did your mum say?' Laurent asked.

I panicked. 'What do you mean?'

'About the bike?'

'Oh. She didn't see it,' I said dismissively.

She had seen it. She had started to say something on her way out the door, but I had looked up from my bowl of cereal and said, 'Don't.' She had paused. We'd stared at each other, the muddle of unexplained half truths about the past like a giant wedge between us. She had left for work without a goodbye.

My fingers were shaking as I went to unchain the bike. I couldn't get the key in the lock. I stopped for a second to compose myself, and my eye caught the flame hair of Rollo Cooper-Quinn jogging past with the cricket squad.

'Gooood work, Laurent!' Rollo shouted with a massive grin on his face.

Laurent gave him a warning look, like he was ruining it for him. I thought of my mum. I thought of everyone at school finding out we might be brother and sister while thinking we were an item.

I was so flustered I dropped my key.

Laurent bent to pick it up at the same time I did. We ended

up nose to nose, our lips mere centimetres apart. I could see the creased smile in his eyes, the few freckles on his cheeks. He reached his hand up as if to cup my face and draw me towards him and kiss me again. And I found myself wanting him to do it. His face was so heartbreakingly handsome, his mouth so so close . . .

An image of Coco flashed before me, sneering with disgust. The reality hit me and I recoiled, jerking back. 'You might be my brother,' I stumbled out.

Laurent dropped his arm like I'd burnt him. 'What?'

I stood up. 'My mum told me last night.'

'Jesus Christ!' Laurent raked a hand through his thick blond hair as his brows drew into a frown. 'How the hell does that work?'

My heart was racing. What had I done? It wasn't my secret to tell and now I'd blurted it out to Laurent, of all people. I tried to act nonchalant, like I didn't care. 'Some one-night stand. Your dad, my mum.'

Laurent was trying to piece it together. 'How do they know each other?'

'From school. My parents went to Chelsea High too.'

Laurent looked confused. 'My parents met at Chelsea High. They've been together ever since.' Then he thought. 'Well, well. Sounds like my dad's been a bit of a naughty boy.'

I flinched at the image of Titus Summers in bed with my mum. 'You can't tell him,' I said, thinking of my own dad, how this would destroy him. 'Please?'

Laurent looked away, out through the school gate. After a moment, he said, 'And what about us?'

'There is no *us*,' I said.

'Seriously?'

'Laurent, we're interchangeable to you,' I said, sweeping my arm to indicate womankind.

As if on cue, the head girl, Juniper Carrington, a willowy redhead from the Upper Sixth, sashayed past and gave Laurent a little wave. Laurent threw her a wink.

'See?' I shook my head. 'You'll just move on to someone else. That's how you work. This isn't about us. There is no *us*. This is about –' I grappled for the right words. 'More than just some stupid kiss.'

He seemed to think about what I said, really letting it soak into his brain. The look on his face made me remember a second ago the desperate craving of my body for him to kiss me. The catch in my throat when our lips had met last night.

I inhaled sharply.

Laurent blinked. 'Yeah,' he said at last. 'Yes, you're right.'

'I know,' I said, pushing away the unexpected tug of disappointment. Remembering that life was just a game for Laurent Summers. Although I'd just been using him too. Hadn't I?

The last of the cricket squad jogged past. The sun dipped behind a white fluffy cloud, so different from the storm last night. A crow eyed us from the gatepost.

Laurent handed me my bike key. 'So what now, sis?'

CHAPTER TWENTY-FOUR

The sun sparkled in puddles on the pavement. Traffic blocked the side street, delivery drivers on mopeds wove between taxis. A couple of Chelsea High kids cycled the wrong way down the one-way street.

Laurent held the iron gate open for me. 'My mum's reaction could be vaguely appealing,' he mused as the metal gate clanged shut behind us. 'She'll go insane.'

I frowned, pushing my bike along the pavement. 'You can't tell her. You can't tell anyone. Promise you won't.'

Laurent looked noncommittal.

'We'll find out if it's true or not. There are tests you can do. I looked it up on the internet.' I could hear the plea in my voice.

I knew exactly how Laurent's brain worked. If he did this for me, I'd owe him. He half smiled and shrugged. 'OK.'

As if it were nothing. In his family, it probably was. The world was probably scattered with the illegitimate children of Titus Summers. I shuddered. My dad had his faults, but at least he was kind.

As we rounded the corner to the main entrance of the

school, one of the younger girls came over, all neat and sweet with pigtail plaits and carrying a giant cello case post orchestra practice. 'Are you Norah Whittaker?' she asked.

I nodded. I'd never seen her before in my life.

The girl handed me a box. 'This is for you.'

'What is it?' I asked, turning over the palm-sized white leather box in my hand.

'That man asked me to give it to you.' She pointed towards the pavement where gaggles of Chelsea High students were loitering and cars idled for pick-up. 'Oh, he's gone.'

I felt my heart start to thrum. 'What did he look like?'

'I can't remember,' the girl said. 'Sorry.' A horn sounded. 'I've got to go. There's my mum.'

She disappeared into a flashy white Lexus. The road was a steady stream of traffic and the pavement crowded. It was impossible to make out a stranger who might have handed the girl the box to give to me.

Laurent nudged my shoulder. 'Come on, open it.'

Daniel and Mr Benson were standing by the railing, conversing over Variety Show notes on a clipboard. 'Norah,' Daniel shouted. 'There's still time to audition!'

I faked a smile, the box burning a hole in my hand.

Coco wafted out in a cloud of curls, Verity by her side. She paused when she saw Daniel and Mr Benson, had a chat about something and giggled. I wondered if she'd bagged the starring role.

I knew whoever had given the girl the box had to be watching from somewhere. I felt on show, conspicuous.

Getting bored, Laurent snatched the box from my hand.

'Give it back!' I tried to grab it from him.

He laughed, holding it high above his head. 'Don't you want to know what's inside?'

'Give it back!' I shouted, causing a few heads to turn. I saw Coco frown.

'Only if you show me what's inside.' Laurent grinned, holding it behind his back, knowing I wouldn't try and grab it now people were watching.

'OK,' I muttered.

Just as I was about to take it, he said, 'I don't trust you,' and snapped the box open himself.

I gasped. Laurent whistled.

Inside the box was a ring, with a flower made of bright yellow stones and sparkling white ones. They glinted in the sunlight so exquisitely they had to be diamonds. Big ones. Mounted on what I presumed was gold. I didn't know the value of what was in Laurent's hand, but it wasn't small change.

Laurent passed it over to me. 'Wow,' he said. 'If that's Ezra's means of apology, then respect to the guy.'

I knew it wasn't from Ezra.

The diamonds reminded me of the sly glint in Vincent Blake's eye. Normal people would send priceless jewels via some specially tracked delivery service, not undercover outside school. But why was Vincent giving me diamonds? Was it stolen? Was it a bribe? I could almost hear him. '*Chop, chop, Norah.*'

Coco came trotting over, same catlike expression as Laurent's, face tight with displeasure. 'What's going on?'

I snapped the box shut. 'Nothing.'

'A love token, from our boy, Ezra,' said Laurent. His lips tilted in a malicious grin, goading his sister. 'Jealous?'

Coco scoffed, one brow arched. 'Please.'

I looked down at the pavement, avoiding eye contact with Coco. My cheeks were burning. It was all too much. The mention of Ezra made my chest tighten. I wanted to take the diamonds and run.

The Summers' dark green Range Rover cruised up to the curb, Wilson the chauffeur at the wheel, Titus in the front passenger seat on the phone. The sight of him made me flinch. He didn't even look up as Coco slid into the back seat.

'You should get in, you're one of the family,' Laurent whispered to me with a sly smile.

I couldn't trust him. That connection had gone. Laurent had other ways of winning now.

'You promised you wouldn't say anything,' I urged him.

'I never promise anything, Norah.'

'Laurent, get in,' Titus barked. 'What happened at practice? Who scored? What were the times?'

And like that they were gone.

When I got home I stashed the ring in my sock drawer, my hands trembling to be rid of it. Then I emailed my dad, asking him to phone me. I had no idea when he'd get the message. And prison queues for the telephone were always long.

My mum wasn't home. She sent a message saying that she hoped to be back by nine, when we could *have a good talk*.

We didn't have good talks any more.

The only person I wanted to talk to was Ezra. I could imagine him listening and understanding and saying something that would make it all right. But when I thought of Ezra now, I saw Coco. And when I thought of Coco, I thought of her maybe being my sister. And then I thought about Laurent, and remembered that I'd kissed him. And there was too much wrong with that to know where to start. No, I couldn't talk to Ezra.

I had Weetabix for dinner again and tried to watch TV but couldn't concentrate. I went for a run instead. My legs were still exhausted from the earlier circuit training and I knew it would be better to let my muscles rest, but I pushed on all the same. The weather was better, the sun still bright as I pounded over the bridge.

Halfway home, on the other side of the river, I hit the wall, barely able to lift one leg after the other like my feet were cased in concrete. I had to stop. I had no money with me and no water. Dusk was blurring the sky as the sun dipped behind the trees, the earlier brightness just a summer's evening illusion.

As I stood there, gasping and woozy, my phone rang. A mobile number I didn't recognise.

'Hello?'

'Norah, sweetheart.' It was my dad.

'How are you calling me? Is this the prison phone?' I asked, still panting for breath, looking for a bench but not finding one so leaning against the river railing.

'Funny thing, I got your email and one of the guys here very kindly said I could use their mobile. It was fate. Oh, hang on. We're not allowed phones so I, er – might have to keep stopping. No it's OK. Fine. Thanks, mate –' I imagined Dad giving whoever was on lookout for the guard the thumbs up.

I suddenly had the feeling of being watched, too vulnerable in my state of exhaustion. Every shadow seemed to move.

'Dad, what if you get caught?' I said.

'It's fine,' my dad replied. 'This lot all know what they're doing. They never get caught.'

'Dad,' I said, talking really quietly, on edge. 'Vincent Blake came to see me.'

There was a pause. 'He did?'

I looked down over the railing at the murky river water below me. The sweat drying on my skin made me shiver. 'And today some stranger gave me a box with a diamond ring in it. I don't know, but I think it's stolen.'

He sounded confused. 'I don't understand. Why would someone –'

There was another pause.

'Dad?'

'Hang on, sweetheart . . .'

My phone battery was running low and I heard it bleep. 'Dad, what do I do?'

He exhaled, deep and worried. 'I don't know. I'm trying to think.'

'Don't think, just tell me what's going on. My battery's running out. I need to know what to do.'

'How would I know?' He sounded stressed.

I ran a hand through my sweaty hair, anxious, aware of how little time we had. Below me the river swirled petrol-grey. 'Dad, Vincent said you owe him a favour,' I said. 'He wants me to persuade you to do whatever it was he wants you to do. Dad, I don't know, but I think the ring is some kind of warning.'

There was silence on the other end of the line.

'Dad,' I said. 'Are you still there?'

My dad muttered, 'Damn. Has he spoken to anyone else? To your grandparents?'

'They're away in the Galapagos Islands. Why? What does Vincent want you to do? What's going on?'

Someone walked really close past me with their hood so far up I couldn't see their face. I pressed my back against the railings. My battery was bleeping. Someone called something to my dad in the background.

'What's the favour?' I urged.

I sensed the change in him. The shutting down. 'It's nothing, Norah honey,' Dad said. 'Nothing to worry about.'

'Of course it's something to worry about!'

Standing there, staring down at the bleak restless river, I wondered who this man was. I wished for my old dad back. For a dreadful moment, I realised I didn't want this one. I wanted the funny man. The hero. The dopey sweet one. I didn't want to deal with this. I didn't want him to be the type of person to drag us all into his mess again.

For one tiny, niggling second I thought of the DNA test that might prove we weren't related at all. I turned my back on the river, hating myself for even thinking that.

'I've got to go,' my dad said. 'Pete needs his phone back. Look, Norah, I'll sort it. I promise. Just – keep it between us, yeah?'

'Yes,' I said reluctantly.

'Thanks, honey.' Then, almost as if the previous conversation had never happened, he added, 'Did you audition for the Variety Show?'

'No!' I snapped, alone, scared and shivering.

'Oh,' he replied, disappointed.

And my phone cut off.

CHAPTER TWENTY-FIVE

I walked home in a trance, checking over my shoulder, flinching at shadows. I had to keep stopping to replay the conversation in my head, coming up with more and more terrifying things Vincent Blake might want my dad to do in order to repay this so-called favour. What would happen if Blake wasn't repaid? I felt the panic course through my body with nowhere to go.

It was quarter to nine. Mum would be home soon, and I'd have to tell her. This was bigger than I could handle on my own. I remembered how she'd looked the night before, so vulnerable and sad. This would only make things worse. But the relief of deciding to tell her alleviated some of my fear. So much so, I found the energy to jog the last bit back to the boat, down the dusky darkness of the jetty to the soft yellow lights of home.

'Mum!' I threw open the door and dashed inside.

The sound of raised voices pulled me up short, skidding like a dog in a cartoon. Ahead of me by the kitchen counter was my mum, looking tight-faced and furious. Across from her was Titus Summers, hands on his hips, cheeks red with barely suppressed anger, still wearing his impeccably cut work suit but with his tie gone and top button undone.

Sitting on one of the small dining chairs was Laurent, head slightly bowed. His hair was damp and he was wearing black tracksuit bottoms, a white T-shirt and flip-flops, like he'd just got out of the shower. And worse than that, next to him was Coco. She sat with her legs crossed, prim and impervious. Her big, wide, innocent eyes triumphant.

Laurent didn't look up.

My breath caught sharp in my throat.

'Where have you been?' Mum said, slow and controlled. 'I've been calling and calling.'

I swallowed. 'My phone died.'

'That's not good enough, Norah,' she said curtly. Coco shook her head in sycophantic agreement.

'The whole claim is outrageous,' Titus interjected, impatient to resume his tirade. 'The idea that I've fathered your child.'

Oh god, he knew. Of course he knew. Why else were they here? I felt faint, white like all the blood had drained out of me.

'It's malicious gossip. I can sue you for slander, you know that don't you, Lois?'

My mum exhaled, tired. 'Titus, you've got the wrong end of the stick.'

Her face was pale, making the grey under her eyes even starker. Her hair was pulled back and all her make-up had worn off. Titus on the other hand looked overbearing and powerful.

I tried to catch Laurent's eye but he wouldn't meet my gaze. In that instant, I hated him so much. 'I can't believe you –' I began.

'What can't you believe?' Coco cut in with a sneer.

'Coco,' Laurent started, but wearily, as if he'd already had enough of the subject.

Coco just kept going, talking over him. 'That you can make up this crap? That you're so petty you're trying to drag our family name through the mud because of what happened between me and Ezra?'

'What?' Only Coco could make this all about herself. 'It's got nothing to do with you and –'

Coco snorted. 'Don't even try, Norah. You're pathetic!'

My mum held up a hand. 'I will not have a slanging match. We can discuss this like adults.'

Titus pushed his jacket back and slid his hands in his trouser pockets. I recognised Laurent in his cocky authority. 'Who do you think you are, telling *my* daughter to behave like an adult?' he said acidly. 'Some slag I barely remember from school who needs a bit of cash because her husband's in the slammer.'

I physically flinched at the word slag. Laurent's eyes shot up, startled.

Mum stood completely still. I could barely see her breathing. The silence hovered in the room like a billion fat bluebottles, heavy and disgusting. I saw the change in her, saw her eyes as they narrowed, her breath as it slowed, like a snake rising up to become a dragon.

'What did you call me?' Her voice was cool and calm and terrifying.

Titus tilted his chin and shrugged, like it didn't need repeating. 'That's not the point.'

I knew Laurent could sense the change too. The atmosphere chilled and sharpened at the same time.

'How dare you come on to my property and insult me and my family. How dare you threaten to sue me . . .' Mum gave a mirthless laugh. 'You're not going to sue me, Titus. Because then I might have to tell Lavinia about all the little games you played when you wanted me but couldn't have me.'

Titus scoffed. 'All I remember is how jealous you were. Jealous of my money. You were with that deadbeat.' They were facing off like wild cats. 'As I remember it, Lois, you were begging.'

My mum absorbed the words like blows. Me, Laurent and Coco watched in silence.

Mum's eyes emanated rage. 'Get the hell off my boat,' she snarled. 'And if I see you here again, if you insult me or my daughter again, I will destroy you and your marriage.'

Titus curled his lip, as if the idea were absurd.

'Don't underestimate me, Titus,' Mum said. 'I have every letter, every gift you ever sent me.' It was her turn to wear the smug smile. 'I have every desperate plea you made in writing – even the telegram you sent on the evening of your wedding. Remember?'

Titus was breathing heavily through his nose like a racehorse.

My mum's eyes were fixed on his. 'When you don't trust someone, Titus, you tend to save the evidence. Now get off my property before I call the police.'

Titus stood for a second, silent, then cleared his throat. 'You're delusional,' he muttered but with less authority than before. 'Coco, Laurent, come on. Time to go.'

Laurent jumped up without looking at me. I felt like I had never known him. Coco trotted behind.

At the door, Titus turned back. 'You'll be hearing from my lawyer about a DNA test. I intend to have this fiasco cleared up as discreetly and quickly as possible.'

Mum stood where she was, face rigid. 'I completely agree, Titus.'

I waited for something from Laurent – for him to turn back, to look, to acknowledge how awful his dad had been, how ashamed he felt. But the three of them left without looking back. Them against us.

When the door slammed, Mum slumped like a rag doll on to one of the dining chairs. I heard her quietly sob – saw the gentle shuddering of her shoulders, her hair hanging over her face. I didn't know what to do.

I started to say, 'I asked Laurent not to . . .' but Mum shook her head like it didn't matter. I fetched her a tissue, pushed it into her hand.

She held it to her eyes, catching her breath. 'There are some things,' she said, voice a hiccup, 'that I need to clarify. I never begged, Norah.'

I shook my head too, close to tears myself.

'I made a mistake,' she went on, wiping her eyes. 'Once. Things with your father at the time were not good. But it was my mistake. And whatever happens,' she said, blowing her nose, gathering her strength, 'your father does *not* need to know.'

I'd have agreed to anything she wanted. But I felt the pressure of secrets weighing heavy, and the bedrock of my family cracking before my eyes. I brought her a cup of tea. And a custard cream. Which annoyingly reminded me of Laurent.

And of Vincent. And of the diamond ring.

I couldn't tell Mum now.

Instead I made her a hot-water bottle and said, 'You should go to bed.'

CHAPTER TWENTY-SIX

The next day at school I had a free last period where we could either do yoga in the Wellbeing room, go to the Variety Performance rehearsal, or study in the library. I chose the darkness of the library, the blinds drawn against the sun, and googled the diamond ring on the school computer. Somehow it seemed less incriminating than using my own phone. That was the type of logic I'd inherited from my dad.

After various false starts, I discovered a grainy photo of a canary-yellow ring resembling the one in my sock drawer, which was part of a collection stolen from an ancestral estate in Marlborough two weeks earlier. The robbery was thought to be linked to another earlier in the year of a chateau in the South of France, by a gang referred to by French police as the *Toile d'Araignée*: the Spider's Web. No beginning, no end, just a network of sticky, inescapable threads. I wondered if Vincent was the spider.

I zoomed in on the photo. My heart was pounding so loudly it surprised me that people couldn't hear it in the dusty quiet of the room. The ring was part of treasures valued at one point three million pounds. And it was in my sock drawer.

I stared at the screen, at the bits I'd glossed over in search of the ring. The detailing of the old couple tied up in their bed, guns held to their heads by men in black masks. The barking dog silenced forever.

The old couple reminded me of my grandparents. I imagined my granddad forced to tell intruders where the safe was, a gun to my grandmother's temple, heartbreakingly powerless. I thought of Ludo their lovely, batty Labrador.

I heard the librarian, Mrs Wells-Jones, doing the rounds so I quickly closed the search window. I felt like eyes were watching me from everywhere.

Suddenly my phone trilled out in the silence of the room.

Mrs Wells-Jones's eyes darted across. 'No phones!' she ordered.

I fumbled with it. The number was withheld. The chance it might be Dad made me scrape back my chair and dash out the room to answer it.

'Hello?' I said, walking fast down the corridor, past the Great Hall and towards the changing rooms. We weren't allowed to use our phones in school during the day. I clutched the handset to my chest, covering it as best I could with my hand, wishing it was winter and I had my jumper sleeves.

Through a crack in the Great Hall doors I could see Coco on stage belting out a jazz number for the Variety Performance. Freddie, Emmeline's brother, came tap-dancing out to join her for the *La La Land* routine, a beautifully choreographed crowd-pleaser. I put my head down and hurried past.

The changing rooms were empty. One of the overhead lights flickered. It was hot and muggy, the windows open to let in some air after whichever class had changed in here before break. There was dry mud on the floor and it smelt of sweat and old kit and damp from the showers. Someone had forgotten their pants.

I sat in the corner on the wooden bench. 'Hello, sorry.' I caught my breath, waiting for my dad to say something.

'Norah, it's Ezra.'

'Oh god.' I tipped my head back against the wall. It was so nice to hear his voice. For a second I felt it course through me, warm and familiar like a hug. But too quickly my brain remembered that it was a sound, like the Variety Performance, not currently on my frequency.

'I'm sorry –' he started.

'I can't do this.' I shook my head. A fat bumblebee was walking slowly along the edge of the flickering light.

'Please don't hang up.'

Something in his voice made me pause. Outside I could hear laughter, the scraping of boots and the kicking of a ball.

'Why not?' I said.

'Because I need to talk to you. Josh had his operation and it went wrong, Norah.'

I saw a flash of little Josh playing Fortnite in his room, his green pyjamas, his beaming smile. 'Oh my god, what happened?'

Ezra exhaled. 'It's not good. They've had to put him in a coma, medically induced, and –' His voice wavered. 'I don't know . . .'

I nodded. Wiped the moisture from my eyes with the back of my hand.

I could hear him breathing. 'I know I really hurt you. You never have to talk to me again. But I just need someone to talk to today.' He paused. 'Not someone. You. I need you to talk to today.'

My heart actually ached for him, like a physical pain. The bumblebee had gone. I looked around and found it on its back on the floor, legs flailing, unable to right itself, wings thrumming on the cold tiles. Round and round it went on its back.

'OK,' I said. I couldn't say no. I quashed the feeling of guilty relief that we had been given a reprieve. A moment out of time where we were allowed to be one.

I picked a leaf up from the changing-room floor that had come in on someone's boot and flipped the bumblebee over. It buzzed immediately up to the light, thirsty for more.

Ezra started to tell me what had happened in the hospital: the sudden rushing of the doctors, the beeping of machines, the terror on his mum's face. And I felt for him. The tremor in his voice. The fear. I imagined if we were lying side by side, how I might trace the side of his face with my finger. How we might wrap ourselves in the grey woven blanket on his bed.

How his dog, At-At, might snuggle his way between us.

His voice cracked. 'Norah, I don't know if he's going to get better this time. I don't know what to do.'

I closed my eyes. I wanted to make it OK for him. I wanted to help him. But my reserves of hope were bled dry. 'I don't know what to say.'

On the other end of the phone, Ezra sighed. 'There's nothing anyone can say, I don't think. I just . . . I just wanted to hear your voice.'

I wrapped my arm round my knees. Weirdly, it helped to hear his voice too. I felt the tug of the invisible thread that tied us. 'You just have to be there for him and wait,' I said.

It was silent. Then he said quietly, 'I can't go in the room.'

I imagined his brother lying there, small and vulnerable, sleeping while machines bleeped. 'You have to,' I said, wishing I was there, wishing I could hold Ezra's hand and lead him in. 'You have to sit there and read him all those comics he likes as if he's awake. As if you have to make him laugh.'

'I can't.' I imagined Ezra sitting with his head in his hand. Thick black lashes closed.

'You can,' I insisted. 'Ezra, I know you. You can. It's Josh. He needs you.'

'He asked me if he should have the op. I didn't know what to say. He looked so hopeful. I said I didn't know. How lame is that? I should have said no.'

'No one can predict the future, Ezra. You did what you thought was right at the time,' I said. Wondering how that applied to the rest of us. My dad, my mum. Me.

Neither of us spoke for a bit. I knew he was listening, though, so I carried on. 'You've been here before. You know that when things get bad, sometimes they get better again.' The words stuck in my throat because I wasn't sure any more if they were true. But for Ezra's sake I repeated them. 'They can, Ezra. Quite often they get better again.'

There was no sound except the thud of the bumblebee hitting the milky glass case of the overhead light.

After a second Ezra said, 'Yeah.' Then, a little more convincingly, 'Yes, you're right. Thank you.'

There was another pause. He laughed softly and added, 'Do you think that'll be the same with us?'

I wasn't expecting the question. Unprepared to fight how much I missed him. Ezra had been my escape. My safe place. I loved him. I hated what he had done but I missed him, and in that moment I didn't understand why *his* mistake had to make *me* unhappy. Why couldn't I just forget about it?

'It was the stupidest thing I've ever done, Norah. You were – are – the best thing in my life.'

I could just forgive him. I could forgive him and then I could tell him everything. Share everything I was feeling inside. I wrapped my arm tighter round my shins and rested my forehead on my knees.

There were new voices outside the window. I recognised one as being Yannis.

'That was a dirty move you pulled out there!'

'You think *that* was dirty?' Laurent's trademark condescension. 'You played like a baby.'

'Screw you.'

'Score some goals and then act like the tough guy,' Laurent drawled.

I flattened my back against the wall. I had kissed Laurent. A memory flashed of the boat, his head bent, the spark like lightning as our lips touched. I squeezed my eyes shut.

Ezra said, 'Norah? Do you think things could get better for us?'

I would have to tell him. Would he forgive me? We weren't together, but it still felt like a betrayal. I had given Laurent the upper hand. He knew more about me now than Ezra did. Just as Ezra had done with Coco. Secrets were power.

'Honestly, Ez, I don't know,' I said, my voice loud in the darkness. 'It's too complicated at the moment. Let's just –' I felt like the bumblebee on its back. 'Let's just focus on Josh. I'll be here for you.'

'OK,' he said. 'That's enough for me.'

When he hung up, I sat clutching my phone, wishing I was back in New York, my head tucked tightly into Ezra's shoulder. Back before none of this ever happened.

The changing-room door banged open.

'Oh, sorry,' said Laurent. 'Didn't realise anyone was in here.'

'Laurent, this is the girls' changing room!'

'I just came in for a piss. Closer than the boys. What are you doing?'

His face was all sweaty, his hair slicked back. After the showdown with his dad last night and his skulking exit, Laurent was the last person I wanted to talk to.

'I was just on the phone,' I said, surreptitiously rubbing under my eyes for possible mascara stains and standing up to leave.

Laurent held out a hand to stop me as I walked past. 'Norah? I didn't mean to tell him. We were arguing and . . . well. You know?'

I looked blankly at him. 'No, I don't know.'

'Well, think back to when you told me,' he said wryly. 'Clearly neither of us is very good at keeping secrets in the heat of the moment.'

I looked away.

Laurent's voice softened. 'I'm sorry I told him.'

'And are you sorry he barged into my home and insulted my family and my mum and was generally an arsehole?' I said.

Laurent's brow creased. 'You can't blame this all on my dad. He's just trying to protect his family.'

'Funny way of showing it.'

'What else was he meant to do?' Laurent seemed bemused. 'Suppose your mum *is* lying?'

I narrowed my eyes, incensed. 'She's not lying.'

'How do you know? Like my dad said, she's in a position to –'

'Stop!' I held up a hand. 'Stop, Laurent.'

He stopped, frowning.

It was all so pointless. I'd just been on the phone talking about a ten-year-old boy lying in a hospital room fighting for his life. How did this compare? Laurent seemed pathetic, his argument condescending and selfish. I was angry at myself for ever feeling anything for him.

'You act like you're so strong,' I said calmly, 'yet you said nothing last night. You couldn't even look at me. Everything you do is for your own self-interest. You use people. You play games. Your father's a bully. So is your sister. And so are you.'

He watched me like I was an opponent on the field. I didn't care. He could play any move he liked. I was done.

I walked closer to him. I could smell his sweat and the mud. 'You think we're after your fortune?' I said. 'You think we're trying to blackmail you? Well, I'll tell you one thing for nothing, Laurent Summers.' I was so close to him now I could see each individual eyelash. 'I wouldn't want to be part of your family for all the money in the world.'

CHAPTER TWENTY-SEVEN

I cycled fast and furious back to the boat, weaving through traffic with a death wish. Cars honked their horns at me; a bus clipped the back of my tyre, making me wobble, but I stayed upright. This was war.

I skidded down the planks of the jetty without getting off my bike. Our French neighbour, Maurice, shouted at me. I swore back, something I'd never done. *Don't give them any ammo*, my mum always warned, but it didn't make any difference.

'I will report you!' he shouted.

'Good!'

I chucked my bike against the railing. No one was home. No one was ever home. The boat was dark and smelt damp from the sun-dried rain.

I marched through with no purpose, just anger and frustration. I was starving. There was nothing in the fridge, as usual. I banged about to see if there was anything in any of the cupboards but they were empty. Then I noticed the slim window in the far corner of the living room, the exact spot where I'd kissed Laurent, was slightly ajar. We never opened that window because the wood had expanded and it was really difficult to close it.

My skin tingled. Someone had been on the boat. I thought of the Spider's Web gang in France, with all its invisible threads. Vincent Blake ready to pounce.

I closed the kitchen cupboard and backed away, peering round to check the rest of the main room was clear. Then I crept in the direction of my bedroom. I carefully unhooked the medieval stunt axe from the wall, feeling the cool weight of it in my hand.

My room had been ransacked. All my things rummaged through and discarded. The snow globe Ezra had given me was smashed on the floor. My books were lying broken and trodden on. All my drawers were open. I went straight for my sock drawer to check on the diamond ring. Of course, the box was gone.

Someone had been in our home. Strangers had gone through my things.

I put down the stunt axe. Attempting to remain calm and normal, I grabbed some clothes from the drying rail, quickly pulling on my threadbare turquoise tracksuit bottoms and a white ribbed vest. I splashed my face with water from the kitchen sink and slipped on my old yellow Converse. I had to get off the boat. I took my books out of my school bag, stuffed a jumper in instead, checked I had my money, keys and phone, then walked out the door as fast as I could.

I was well out of my depth.

Back on my bike, I hurtled up the jetty – more shouts from Maurice – and hit the main river road. Why had they taken the ring? Had my dad agreed to Vincent's favour?

I found myself at Clapham Junction, locking up my bike. My body had known where I was going before I'd realised it myself. As I sat on the train, then the bus, every eye seemed to be looking at me. But finally I was at the river, and Mulberry Island was in front of me in all its perfect hidden-away glory. The willow trees licking the surface of the glassy river. The twinkling lights of the pub garden. The tall cedars. The crumbling boathouses.

I ducked on to the overgrown path that skirted the edge of the island. The smell of the place was like walking back into my childhood.

Jess's house was a tiny white bungalow with a Spanish tiled roof. I reached it just as she was coming out the front door. I felt my body soar at the sight of her.

'Norah?' She stopped with surprise. 'What are you doing here?'

She had an expression on her face like she knew exactly why I was there. This was always where I ran when things got bad.

'It's all gone wrong,' I said, wryly resigned.

'Again?'

'Again.'

'Norah Whittaker?'

I turned to see a middle-aged man in a black bomber jacket holding up a shiny police badge and a woman with a long coat and neat brown plait.

'I'm Detective Constable Burnley,' he said. 'This is my colleague, Detective Sergeant Martin. We'd like a word.'

I started to tremble.

DC Burnley reached out in a gesture of calm. 'No need to worry, Norah. We're just here for a friendly chat.'

I felt Jess move closer to stand by my side.

'We just want to know if you are familiar with a man called Vincent Blake,' DS Martin said. 'Your father's name has come up in conjunction with his, and so has yours. Vincent Blake is not a good man, Norah. It's very important that you tell us anything you know.'

All I could say was, 'My dad's in jail,' my voice wobbly with panic. Jess's hand reached to clutch mine.

Then suddenly I heard, 'All right, officers, what's going on here?'

Tricky, my dad's old fishing friend, came ambling over, his fishing rod and tackle box in one hand, fold-up seat in the other.

DC Burnley shook his head. 'Nothing for you to worry about, sir. Just a little chat.'

Tricky frowned, big bushy eyebrows drawing together. 'With a minor? No parent or guardian present? You know better than that, officer.'

I felt my heart skip a beat. DS Martin narrowed her eyes.

Tricky stood there, half smiling, while his dark piratical eyes flashed a warning. 'I think you'd better come back when you're in a more official capacity, don't you?'

DC Burnley's eyes searched for a way round this obstacle, but found none. He sighed with frustration. 'Come on,' he said to his colleague. 'Norah, just have a think,' he added.

Tricky held the gate open. 'Go on, off you go,' he said sternly, watching them leave like a Doberman on guard.

'Come on, Norah love, come with me,' he said gently when he was confident they were off the island. 'You're shaking.'

Tricky led us to the rehearsal room at the back of the theatre while he called my mum. There was a piano in the corner with the sheet music of whatever had last been practised and a guitar leaning against the wall. It smelt of cigar smoke and sun-warmed dust.

He made us hot chocolate as we waited. Soon enough, the door swung open, almost off its hinges, and Mum charged in. Her presence in the place was so familiar, and yet so alien.

'Norah?' she said, no pause to take off her jacket, or to say hello to Tricky. 'What the hell's going on?'

I burst into tears. Jess looked like she might cry too. Mum wrapped her arms tight round my shoulders, pressing me close. She smelt of sweat and perfume and fear.

I couldn't keep it in any longer. I told her about Vincent

Blake, the ring, the call from my dad and the promise I wouldn't say anything. The ransacked boat.

My mum looked more and more aghast. 'How do I not know about any of this?'

I shook my head. She knew why. She was never there.

'Why did this Blake guy give you the ring and then take it back?' Jess asked.

Tricky went over to the kettle. 'The police were probably sniffing about. Tea, Lois? Or something stronger?'

'Tea will be fine, thanks, Tricky,' said my mum at the proffered bottle of whisky.

I wiped away the remains of any tears and blew my nose. 'I think Vincent wanted to scare Dad into doing what he wanted by giving us stolen goods –'

Mum cut me off. 'I'm going to kill your father. I'm going to kill him. How could he do this?' She paced the threadbare rug. 'How could he put you in danger?'

Tricky came over with the tea. 'I know it doesn't look good, but don't be too quick to judge Bill.'

My mum gaped.

'Don't look at me like that, Lois,' Tricky said. 'All I'm saying is it's a different world in there, with different rules. I did some time when I was eighteen. Wouldn't go back if you paid me.'

My mum shook her head. 'Bill's not eighteen, Tricky. He's a grown man. He shouldn't lose his sense of right and wrong at the drop of a hat.'

'I doubt he has,' Tricky replied. 'Vincent told Norah that Bill owed them a favour, but Bill probably doesn't even know what for. It could've been anything. It could have been for lending him a bloody toothbrush. Bill doesn't know how it works. They want him to do something, they'll make him do it, favour or no favour.'

Mum looked dubious.

'It's bloody tough, Lois, believe me,' said Tricky. 'Bill's from a rich family and he's soft. He's an easy target.'

'He's a fool,' snapped my mum.

'Yes,' agreed Tricky. 'But he won't have done this on purpose. You know that.'

My mum looked unconvinced. 'Well, we'll see what the police have to say.'

Tricky raised his hands like he'd said his bit. But I was listening. I could envisage the loneliness, the misunderstanding. The new rules, the bullies, the secret codes and the hierarchies. I had been there. I knew what it felt like to be sinking in a new world. You did what you could to survive.

'We're not going to the police,' I said. 'We have to give Dad the chance to handle this.'

My mum stared at me, incredulous.

'We have to remember who he is,' I said. 'That we're on his side.'

'This isn't a game, Norah. It's serious.'

I tried to keep my voice even, to stand my shaky ground.

'That's why we have to trust him. If he needs our help, he'll ask for it. We can't assume that we know better. I met the police, Mum. They are not going to be on Dad's side.'

Tricky said, 'Norah's right on that one.'

Mum started pacing.

'We've all lied,' I said softly. 'We have secrets. We've made mistakes.'

Mum's eyes flared in warning. Our gazes locked.

'We have to give him a chance to solve this,' I went on. 'We have to trust him. Because we would want him to trust us, to give us a chance. Wouldn't we?'

Mum looked down at the fraying rug. Then at Tricky, who gave a simple nod.

'It's such a bloody mess,' Mum sighed.

'Aye,' agreed Tricky. 'That it is.'

The only sound was the humming of the small fridge, until Tricky picked up the guitar in the corner and started to strum a song he'd written with my dad. I remembered it, every word.

Mum did too. She paused her pacing and poured herself a glass of water. She rested against the sink and undid the top buttons of her shirt to get cooler in the warm room.

Tricky started to sing, low and gravelly. Jess half smiled, like old times.

My mum slipped off her shoes so she was barefoot. I could see the red pinched marks her shoes had left. Tricky gestured for her to take up the mic but she rolled her eyes like the idea was preposterous.

Tricky changed song. *Moon River*. Mum's absolute favourite. I remember when she used to sing it to my dad. His mouth spread wide into a smile. He nodded to the mic again. Jess nodded encouragingly.

I watched Mum put the glass down on the side. Think, while Tricky strummed. And then she crossed the room, opened her mouth and sang. She had a voice like honeysuckle. Soft and sweet. It was enough to make you cry.

When the song ended, Mum subtly dabbed her eyes to wipe away a tear. Tricky didn't let the music pause for long, too aware how easily she might walk away.

I sat with Jess on the ratty old sofa, my chin resting in my hands, watching and smiling. It was like slotting back into a memory; a snapshot of nostalgia. My mum looked so relaxed, hair falling in glowing waves, no make-up, eyes closed.

When the song finished, she beckoned me over with her finger. I declined with a shake of my head. I didn't want to sing. I wanted to watch.

My mum widened her eyes like she used to when I was a kid getting a telling-off.

I shook my head again.

She put her hands on her hips and ordered, 'Norah, get over here!'

Tricky laughed. 'Go on.'

'I can't,' I whispered, curling deeper into the chair.

213

Mum looked me straight in the eye. 'Yes you can.'

There was a sensation, as she took my hand and wrapped her fingers round mine tight, that things had changed. That I didn't have to carry this on my own any more. And as I stood up, it felt like I was walking on air. Held by the people around me, the gentle music as Tricky played guitar and Jess moved to the piano. My mum stood at the mic with her hand still holding mine and started the next song, low and soft and mournful.

The hairs on the back of my neck stood on end.

It was impossible not to think of Dad, missing from the room. His smile. His laugh. Impossible not to imagine him alone and afraid in jail. I saw the chasm that separated us. I remembered that he wasn't the bad guy.

As I opened my mouth and sang, the music infused me like ink in water. This was different to playing netball. This wasn't escape. This was presence. This wasn't a fight. It was acceptance. This was pleasure. This was happiness.

Immediately, I felt guilty for doing something I loved while there was so much wrong in our lives.

I felt Mum's hand squeeze mine, and wondered if she felt the same. But it wasn't just guilt I was feeling. It was something else. Fear. Because if I opened the doors and let this in, then who knew what else would come with it?

It was easy to be numb. The fear lay in feeling.

CHAPTER TWENTY-EIGHT

We didn't go to the police.

I slept that night in my mum's bed, the medieval stunt axe beside us, the chest of drawers pushed half over the door. Afraid but together. Cosy, united.

We talked late into the night about what we'd do next. My mum wouldn't quit her job – we needed the money – but she'd cut back the hours and see what happened.

'What do you think they'll say?' I asked, face to face with her on the pillows.

She stroked my hair. 'I don't care what they say.'

We started getting all excited about reviving the Portobello stall and texted Jackie at midnight about it. Jackie immediately wrote back with: *Thank the lord! Finally.*

As I drifted off to sleep, I almost felt peaceful, for the first time in a long while.

We were woken at 7 a.m. by a knock on the door. Terrified that it would be Vincent Blake or the police, it was almost a relief when we found a Harley Street doctor and his assistant on the doorstep with instructions to carry out a DNA test at the request of Titus Summers.

Almost.

As I opened my mouth to have my cheek swabbed, Mum stood in her silk dressing gown, arms wrapped tightly round her waist. All her hatred for Titus Summers was channelled into the venomous look she was giving the doctor.

'Results should be no more than forty-eight hours,' he said.

'I want to know at the same time as Titus,' my mum said.

'Well, there'll be a few minutes in it.' The doctor gave a tight little laugh. 'I only have one pair of hands to make the call.'

'Do you think this is funny?' Mum asked.

The doctor straightened his face. 'Absolutely not.'

I found a missed a call from Ezra on my phone from the middle of the night. Just looking at his name on the screen felt like a different life. I couldn't think about him, or us, right now, so instead I messaged to ask how Josh was getting on.

No change. Thanks for asking. Ez x (I miss you).

I didn't reply.

It was a big week at school with the start of the Inter-School Sports Tournament. Six big rival schools were involved, and matches in all sports were taking place throughout the week, culminating in Finals Friday.

Out of the classroom windows I could see marquees being built on the car park, including a champagne bar, hospitality tent, bandstand for the school orchestra, and prize winners' podium. Friday evening would end in style with the Variety Performance.

It was one of those weeks when people were in and out of school, either playing, rehearsing or practising. Half the teachers hated the disrupted lessons, but had to feign solidarity for the school. Nothing was more important at Chelsea High than success.

Polo was the biggest sport, and got the loudest cheers when head boy Rory Fitzgerald read out the results at the end of the day – mainly because both the boys' and girls' teams were reigning champions, and we had Laurent, who apparently had a handicap similar to some of the top-ranked players in the world and was something of a polo celebrity.

On Monday morning, Malaika and I hovered around the netball noticeboard to see who had made the final cut. I was pleased to have something tangible to focus on again. Something with rules and regulations.

'I'm going to be reserve, I think,' Malaika said.

'I don't think you'll be reserve. I'll be reserve,' I replied, hopping apprehensively from one foot to the other.

As I saw Ms Stowe marching round the corner with the team list flapping in her hand and Bettina trotting alongside, I had to admit that I cared. That was the problem with allowing oneself to feel things. I had trained so hard, and I found that I really wanted it now. I wanted it for me.

Ms Stowe reached for a drawing pin and stuck her piece of

paper up on the board, smoothing it flat with her sport-worn fingers. It read:

– Goal shooter – Malaika Zakari

– Wing defence – Norah Whittaker

The thrill when I saw my name shot sparks through my skin. I had been chosen. I had made it. It pushed all other thoughts out of my mind, and handed me something solid.

Ms Stowe gave us a stern look. 'Don't let me down.'

I wondered if my smile was as wide as Malaika's.

We played the first away game that afternoon and won by two goals, the team coming together in perfect sync, Malaika and I working extra hard to prove our worth. Buoyed by that win, we also won the second game straight after, this time by the skin of our underdog teeth.

It was weird coming back to the boat to find the lights on and the radio playing. A luxury that lifted my spirits even further, and the best start to a week I'd had all term.

'I'm trying to arrange a visit to your dad's on Saturday,' Mum said as we ate Singapore fried noodles with chopsticks while watching TV.

I wondered when we'd starting referring to prison as 'your dad's'. It wouldn't be an easy visit. We'd emailed asking for him to call, but had had no reply. That wasn't unusual, but it sat a little uncomfortably in the back of my mind.

My grandparents were still away. My mum had rung Harold, their butler, just to check that the house was all locked up and the dog safely in kennels. Harold had been more than a little surprised by her concern.

Every time someone knocked on the door or the phone rang, there was a definite air of anxiety, but so far there were no more police. And no more Vincent.

The netball team drew our first game on Tuesday morning, but lost the second. It didn't feel good to lose, but it wasn't a disaster. And because of the first wins, our goal-scoring average placed us in the top half of the scoreboard.

By Tuesday evening, there was still no news about the DNA test. As we ate dinner, my mum flicked through her diary. 'He said forty-eight hours, didn't he?'

As if on cue, her phone rang. But it was Mum's boss, not the doctor. She let it go through to voice message.

'It's nothing that can't wait till the morning,' she said, tucking into the simple pasta dinner she'd made.

Still no word from my dad.

My phone rang next. Ezra.

Mum said, 'Take it. You can heat up your dinner later.'

I snatched up the phone and went to my bedroom. 'Hi,' I said, weirdly nervous, like we were shy strangers again. I perched on the edge of my bed, looking out at the river. 'How's Josh?'

'Better.' I could hear the lightness in Ezra's voice. 'He's not awake yet, but the swelling has gone down and the surgeon seem happier. It's an improvement.'

'Oh, that's good,' I said, feeling his relief.

After a moment's pause, he asked, 'How are you?'

'Fine,' I said, too quickly. With Josh on the mend, the truce was over. Everything that was wrong between us flooded back in.

Ezra was clearly aware of the tension. 'Well, I just wanted to tell you that, about Josh. And I wanted to say thanks. I know things are, you know, not totally right between us, so I won't push my luck.'

He tested a laugh. I felt myself smile on instinct. I tried to hold on to the moment, to ignore the past and the future, and just imagine his face with its beautiful lopsided grin.

Silence again.

'I miss you, Norah,' Ezra said.

I found myself nodding. It was so confusing.

'Well,' he said awkwardly. 'I'd better go. I'm at the hospital. I just wanted you to know.'

He hung up. I sat holding the phone, trying to remember the perfection of my trip to New York, what it had felt like to have his arm tight around me as we walked, like nothing else mattered in the world as long as we were together. But it was just out of reach. The memory felt like someone else's life. A different me.

CHAPTER TWENTY-NINE

On Wednesday afternoon, we won the fifth game of the tournament and lost the sixth. Our goal-scoring average ranked us in forth position in the results table. We still had a chance, because fourth place put us in the second semi-final on Thursday which, if we won – against the highest-scoring team – would get us a place in the final. This was something a Chelsea High netball team had never achieved before. Everyone was buzzing.

The news elicited some cheers when announced by head girl, Juniper Carrington, though didn't reach the wild crescendo of the polo score as Laurent himself swaggered on to the stage to announce their still unbeaten record. I wanted him to search me out in the crowd, so I could give him a look of total disinterest. But annoyingly he didn't.

On the way out of school, I passed Rollo and Emmeline trotting down the main steps together, his arm slung possessively round her shoulders. I gave her a faint smile as I wheeled my bike to the curb. She smiled back. The idea of us ever having had the time to talk to one another felt like a different life. If she wasn't glued to Rollo, she was with Coco and Verity.

'Norah!'

I knew immediately whatever Rollo wanted me for wouldn't be good. I steeled myself.

Rollo grinned. 'Seen the advert? You and Laurent can deny it all you like, but the camera never lies.' He cracked up, along with a couple of the cricket boys who were inevitably following him and Emmeline.

I felt my cheeks flush. The Vox advert. I hadn't seen it. I didn't know it was out.

Without replying, I jumped on my bike and pedalled away. I could hear Rollo's laughter behind me. As soon as I was out of sight, I veered down a side street, got my phone out and found the ad online. Leaning against a warm brick wall, I pressed Play.

'Oh my god,' I whispered as I watched the thirty-second clip.

It was mostly Coco on her swing with Emir. The cuts were of the bonfire and the chase. But interspersed, like a little sub-plot, were cursory glances between me and Laurent. Him looking, wanting. His hand grasping mine as we ran through the dark. His body getting closer to mine as we sat on the velvets, his lips getting closer and closer until he laughed and pulled away. My face flushed with surprise and, I hated to admit it, desire.

The whole thing made me feel ill. I tipped my head back, staring up at the bright blue sky. I thought about Ezra watching it, confused at this additional storyline I'd never mentioned.

I reminded myself it was just acting. No one thought anything was going on between Coco and Emir. Why imply anything more between me and Laurent? Rollo liked to wind people up. We were just playing a part for the cameras.

But the chemistry was undeniable. It leaped off the screen. Burned between us.

He might be my half-brother.

Don't think about it, I warned myself, trying to forget the whole thing as I weaved back into the smoggy traffic. Ezra wouldn't care. It was just acting. My thumping heart however didn't seem to agree.

He might be my brother, I said, over and over in my head, to block out all other thoughts of Laurent.

When I got home, Mum was on the phone. She held her hand up to stop me from saying anything, listening to whoever was on the other end of the line.

'Let me get this right,' she said. 'Titus Summers is *not* Norah's father?' She held her hand to her chest. 'Oh, thank god!'

I sank on to one of the bar stools by the kitchen counter, my limbs suddenly trembling. I shut my eyes, and thought of my dad's face from when I was tiny, twirling me round and round, holding on to my arms, laughing as the world behind him became a blur. I saw him trying to persuade me that spaghetti hoops were worms tied in knots. I saw him lying on the floor of my bedroom when I had a nightmare and couldn't sleep, or combing the nits out of my hair. I saw all the things that made him my dad. I knew being a dad was not all about being biologically related, but I couldn't deny the relief that those cherished everyday elements of my past were locked down, unchanged.

Then, cutting through those memories, I saw Laurent by the window with rain-damp hair, head dipped for his lips to brush mine.

He wasn't my brother.

My eyes flew open.

My mum was watching me, the phone still in her hand. 'I don't think I've ever been more relieved about anything in my life,' she said.

I shook my head. 'Me neither.'

'No need to mention it . . .' she started.

I shook my head. The silent understanding between us that now my dad would never need to know.

On Thursday it poured all night and all morning. Fine, slanting rain like mist. I stared out of the window in Maths, willing the clouds to part and reveal blue sky. Semi-finals day.

Mr Watts slammed his hand on the desk. 'Ms Whittaker, you will not find the answer out there!'

The rain didn't stop. It just slowed, making the game feasible. The other team arrived in their dark green minibus, staring menacingly out of the windows. They'd beaten us when we'd played them earlier in the week.

We were walking out to the court to warm up when I realised I'd forgotten my water bottle and dashed back to the changing rooms to get it.

'All right, Whittaker?'

Laurent was coming out of the boys' changing room. He was in his polo whites. His face was tanned from the sun, his hair blonder. I couldn't deny how attractive he was, but he was still the last person I wanted to see.

'My name's Norah,' I said.

'And thankfully your surname is Whittaker. Not related, eh?' he said, giving my shoulder a nudge. 'That's a stroke of luck.'

'It's good for my family,' I said, haughtily.

He smirked. 'And good for you and me.'

'I've told you, there is no you and me.' I started to walk away in the direction of the netball court.

He jogged to get in front of me. 'You can't deny it, Norah. We've all seen the longing on your face in the advert. Did Ezra like it?'

'Leave me alone,' I said.

Ezra had messaged the night before to say I looked beautiful. He didn't mention the advert itself, or Laurent.

With a chuckle, Laurent fell back into step. 'Admit it. You're pleased we're not related.'

I stopped. Looked at his perfect face, cocky smile, gleaming eyes. 'Yes,' I said. 'I'm glad we're not related. But mainly because I can't imagine anything worse than having Summers blood running through my veins.'

'Whoa.' He held up a hand. 'That's a bit harsh.'

'I haven't forgiven you for the way your dad treated us when he came to the boat,' I spat. 'And I haven't forgiven you for doing nothing about it.'

'That was between my dad and your mum. It wasn't anything to do with me.'

I could see my team doing warm-up runs, so I had to speak quickly.

'I don't get you Laurent,' I said. 'You don't seem to care about anything or anyone that isn't you. You don't care that your dad has affairs. You don't seem to mind that you told him something I'd asked you to keep secret. You didn't acknowledge me at all when you came on the boat because, what? You didn't want your dad to know we were friends? Not that we *are* friends. Then you sat back and said nothing when your dad insulted my mum, even though he insults all of you all the time and I *know* you hate it. I've seen your face when he talks to you. People get hurt all the time because of your family – and you don't do anything about it.'

I watched his face harden. 'Oh, and you're perfect?'

'I didn't say that,' I said. 'You just don't like the truth.'

'Don't like the truth,' he scoffed with the same condescending smirk as his father. 'That's rich coming from you. "*Oh, Ezra, I forgive you, I'll take you back, I'll do anything you want.*" You're the weak one, Norah. You're the fraud.' He leaned really close. 'We kissed. You remember that? You can't block it out.'

In that moment I hated him. 'Laurent, you'd kiss anyone.'

He inclined his head like that might be so. 'But you wouldn't.'

I had no reply. Laurent's eyes sparkled again, like he'd hit the spot.

'You blame me, Norah, but that's total crap. You're just looking for excuses because you can't handle the fact that you like me more than Ezra. And that terrifies you.'

I stared into his green eyes. The blood pounded in my ears.

From the courts I heard a whistle blow and Ms Stowe shout, 'Norah! Get over here! You're late.'

Laurent scratched his jaw, nonchalant. 'Well, good luck with the game,' he said, as if nothing had just happened.

'Well, I hope you lose,' I snapped, jogging towards the netball court.

The last thing I heard was his patronising guffaw.

The game was really tough. The other team were good – they'd proved that in the heats. We pulled ahead a couple of times, but they always equalised and then scored again in quick succession. The light drizzle didn't help, the ball slipping out of our hands or making our trainers skid. But we had the drive to make the final. Bettina kept shouting that we were doing it to make Chelsea High history. For me it was just a simple desire to win. With everyone playing their hearts out by the last quarter, the other team only had a one-goal lead.

I forced myself to stay focused, even though Laurent kept creeping into my mind. His gaze. His accusations. Too late, I thought of a million things I could have said back at him. I itched to run across the field and say them now.

As we went into the last quarter, the headmaster was ambling round the grounds, yakking with his cronies under a giant golf umbrella. They stopped to watch as Malaika scored and we drew level. There was suddenly a chance we might make the final. Re-energised, the pace of the game increased as the clock counted down.

Bettina had the ball poised ready to shoot. I hovered on the edge of the circle, waiting. My eye caught sight of Laurent in the distance, charging round the training ring on his horse. His straight back, the arrogant cut of his silhouette, the cool intensity I knew was in his eyes. The lemon scent. The cocky half-smile. The unadulterated confidence. The pull I felt inside myself whenever he was near. *Did* I like him more? *Was* I glad Ezra had cheated?

'Norah!' Bettina shouted but it was too late. The ball ricocheted off me. I hadn't been concentrating. I'd thought she was going to shoot, not pass back to me. I snapped into focus, but not quick enough.

Play was already up the other end of the court. In a matter

of seconds, the other team had scored the winning goal. The whistle blew. We'd been knocked out, and it was my fault.

Bettina was shooting daggers at me. So was Layla. So was Ms Stowe. But it was the look of disappointment on Malaika's face that really got me.

I heard the headmaster say, 'Semi-finals is perfectly acceptable for these girls. It's as far as Chelsea High netballers usually get, so there's no disgracing the side. All eyes are on the polo. And of course, Laurent Summers.'

I couldn't believe it. I wanted to turn back the clock. Everyone was shaking hands, the opposition beaming. Our team sloped away to the sidelines in damp kit. Anouschka, who'd been on the reserve bench, tried to sound positive, but no one was listening. I could see what they were thinking, and I hated it.

I got home that night to find out Mum had lost her job.

'They didn't appreciate my new work ethic,' she said wryly over a glass of wine, standing by the oven while cooking a stir fry.

'What are we going to do?' I asked.

She chucked a handful of veg into the wok. 'I'll get another job,' she said as if it was nothing. 'And if it comes to it –' She paused, seemed to have trouble swallowing a gulp of wine. 'I'll have to ask your grandparents for help.'

She was doing this for me. She could easily have carried on

in the job she was in. But she had cut down her hours for my sake, and now she was willing to accept hand-outs from the very people she resented in order to stay around for me.

I went over and hugged her, tight round the waist.

'Hey,' she said, laughing, moving away slightly as if unused to the contact.

I didn't let go. Instead, I rested my head on her shoulder. I could feel her heartbeat, smell her perfume. Then to my shame, I found myself crying – sobbing into her black and white striped shirt. I tried to stop, but it was like my body had taken over and wasn't letting go.

'Norah!' My mum pushed me back so she could see my tear-ravaged face. 'It's not that bad. We've been through far worse.'

'I know,' I sobbed. 'But we lost the netball.'

'What netball?' She really knew nothing about my life at the moment.

'The semi-finals,' I said with a hiccup, 'and it was all my fault. But it wasn't my fault, it was Laurent's fault. But it wasn't his fault. It was Ezra's fault. But then it wasn't his fault. He didn't do it on purpose. I don't know –' I was crying again.

My mum took the dinner off the hob and steered me towards the kitchen table, pulling out a chair and sitting me down. I blew my nose and wiped my eyes with the palms of my hands. She sat next to me and waited.

'It's just so hard,' I croaked, looking up at her worried face. 'Relationships.'

She gave a knowing smile of agreement. 'No one's perfect, Norah. Relationships will always have bad bits. But if they're right, they're worth it.'

I looked down at my hands, fiddling with the tissue.

'When I was growing up, I had everything money could buy,' Mum said. She had a sip of wine. 'But I didn't have much love. No one really liked each other in my house. No one ever laughed.'

I tried to imagine her parents, who I'd never met, though once I'd read a tabloid article documenting her millionaire mother's fifth divorce celebration on a super-yacht in Cannes. As she described her family, all I could think of was Coco and Laurent. I wondered how much laughter there was in their home.

My mum went on. 'I think that was what first attracted me to your dad. He made me laugh. He thought life was fun. And we were united by this desire not to be who our parents were. Not to strive for more. To be happy, not rich. That was our motto.' She laughed softly. 'To be happy, not rich,' she said again.

I remembered them dancing barefoot on the island, fairy lights twinkling in the trees. 'And that's what you did,' I said.

'Yes,' she agreed. 'In the end. But it's hard to make big changes in your life. Scary. There's safety on one side, and

231

no safety on the other. You can have big dreams at school, Norah, but when you leave and you're faced with this giant world, it's daunting – especially if you're trying to make it on your own, like Bill and I were. It was harder than we thought it would be, having no money. We'd separated ourselves from our families. It was just the two of us. We lived in a dreadful bedsit with rats in the walls and a vile landlord, and it was the exact opposite of what we were used to. God, we were so naïve.'

I blew my nose again. I realised I was shivering, my clothes still damp, so reached over to grab a sweatshirt I'd left on the other chair.

Mum sorted out two bowls of stir fry and a glass of water for me.

I took a forkful of food. 'What happened?' I asked, mouth full.

'We struggled,' she said with naked honesty. 'We argued. Mostly about money. Your dad went to his parents – your grandparents – and asked for help for some hare-brained scheme without telling me. I got mad. He lost the money. Then he did it again. I got mad again. He did it again, and they refused to bail him out. He got mad that time.' She bit her lip. 'He still wanted to be rich,' she said. 'He wanted to be famous.'

I sipped my water. The apricot light of the late sun flooded into the boat, making our skin glow.

'For a while, we stopped believing in ourselves,' Mum said.

'I was working in the city for a big fashion supplier, all hours, on very little pay. Your dad was trying every way he could to break into acting. He got resentful. I got resentful. And there was no laughter any more. Suddenly, I couldn't remember the reason I was doing this.'

I had a sudden flash of Ezra. We hadn't laughed in weeks.

'And then one day, in the city, I bumped into Titus Summers.' Mum sighed, long and slow, reluctantly wrenching the memory loose. 'Since school, Titus Summers had set his sights on me. I don't think he loved me, but he wanted to have me. He was very good-looking, very charming.'

I thought of Laurent. The thrill of the chase, his desperate desire to win at all costs.

'Anyway, I won't dwell on it, but he insisted on taking me to the Ritz for a drink and then another, then dinner. And I got seduced by it.' Mum pushed her plate away and sat cradling her red wine. 'I made the stupidest mistake I've ever made. I chose my old life.' She tied her hair up high on her head, her expression sad and annoyed. 'I hated myself, and I hated Titus. He was so smug, like he'd won, in this plush room at the Ritz.'

I didn't want to know this stuff, but I sat silently listening.

'I was so disgusted with myself afterwards. I threw up behind a tree in St James's Park. When I got home, your dad didn't ask where I'd been. I don't know what he thought, but me not coming home was certainly a turning point in our lives.

A wake-up call. The next day he came home with a set of keys and said, "I've bought a boat" and it was this rust bucket.'

She gestured round us at our home and smiled properly for the first time. 'First day we took it out, your dad crashed into the bank and water started coming in. We had to moor up and start bailing. These people came to help us, and I remember this old man saying, "Don't worry, we can fix that up in a jiffy." All I could see were these big mulberry trees covered in fruit, and I thought, this place is heaven. This is meant to be my home.'

She stopped, eyes dewy. 'That was how we came to live on Mulberry Island. And then you came along and things got even better.'

She covered my hand on the table with her own. 'I can't even remember now why I was telling you all that.' She paused. 'Oh yes. Relationships are hard. Indeed. They will always have their ups and downs because we humans are sometimes weak and sometimes strong. But a relationship has to be worth it. It's not a duty to be with someone, Norah. And it's never a duty to forgive someone either. On the other hand, nor is forgiveness a weakness.'

I put my head in my hands. 'Urgh! It's so complicated.'

She grinned. 'I love you.'

'I love you too,' I whispered.

And I realised, of all the people that were worth it in my life, right now she was the most important. In that moment

I felt safe and secure, and at peace. That was what love was meant to feel like.

CHAPTER THIRTY

It was Finals Friday. Everyone had the day off lessons and the fields were packed with parents from the six different schools that had been competing all week. The orchestra opened proceedings with Chelsea High's own anthem, all the alumni parents standing with their hands pressed proud to their chests while the current students mumbled half-forgotten words. Champagne from the bar was flowing. There was a stall selling flags in each school colour, and matching bunting was strung over the various fields and courts. Massive Chelsea High banners were pinned on every visible wall.

The headmaster appeared in the back of a black open-topped Range Rover, cruising the edge of the field, doing a slow wave like royalty. The car stopped at the podium and he climbed out. Tapping the microphone to check that it was on, he cleared his throat.

'Ladies and gentlemen, I declare open the seventieth annual Inter-School Sports Tournament finals, proudly hosted by Chelsea High School. Boys and girls, good luck.'

The crowd roared. The head looked pleased with himself.

It was hard to get excited, watching everyone who'd

qualified for the final strutting in their Chelsea High tracksuits. I passed Bettina and Layla standing with the cricketers. They didn't look at me as I passed. Boo Clemency-Hall was sitting on her own on a bench with a sad-looking Chelsea High flag in her hand. Malaika was helping on the scoring committee. That was our netball team, carved up and displaced.

The crowds started cheering as Coco, Verity and Emmeline came jogging out of the changing rooms, fresh-faced and determined in their glistening white kit, ready for the girls' polo final.

Ms Stowe's voice suddenly came over the tannoy system. 'Could the Chelsea High netball team please report to the registration box immediately.'

The scattered members of our team headed in Ms Stowe's direction. She was waiting for us, hands on hips, hair scraped back.

'You're playing, girls,' she said.

'What?' Bettina looked confused.

'The other team have been struck down with food poisoning and aren't going to make it. Your goal average put you in third place. So you're on.' She was trying to look fierce and like she didn't care, but you couldn't miss the little pull of excitement on her lips.

'Oh my god!' Layla whooped.

Boo and Anouschka hugged. Malaika grinned at me. I felt my excitement bubble up to bursting.

'Anouschka, you'll play wing defence,' said Ms Stowe. 'Norah, you'll be on the bench.'

'Oh,' I said, unable to hide my deflation.

'Go and get changed, everyone!' Ms Stowe shouted. Then to me, she said, 'I can't afford to take any chances, Norah.'

I nodded. I was devastated but I understood.

The sun was blazing. The other team were good. Prepped and psyched up, ready. All their parents were in the crowd, supporting with shouts of serious encouragement. In contrast, the Chelsea High team were just bright-eyed and excited. None of our families knew we were playing, so the crowd was mainly our classmates egging us on with wild flag waving and whooping.

As the first quarter got under way, I sat on the bench, watching with fists clenched as we made stupid errors while trying to get into sync. We lacked the focus of the opposition. We passed to the wrong team, missed shots that should have been easy, till we were so far down it felt pointless even trying. Ms Stowe went nuts with her pep talk after the first quarter, but that just seemed to dishearten the team even more.

I didn't know what was worse – not making the final, or losing it by a mile.

By half-time, it looked hopeless. The team slumped on the bench with their water bottles. Ms Stowe was pacing. Half our cheering classmates had drifted away.

Finally, Ms Stowe crouched down so she was on our level. 'You're playing like you shouldn't be here,' she said. Her eyes scanned the line of dejected, hanging heads. 'You're playing like you owe them a win. Look at me!'

Everyone looked up.

'You owe them nothing!' Ms Stowe said, slow and pronounced. 'You are all good enough to be here. You are all special.'

I saw Malaika swallow. Boo sat up a bit straighter.

'You have a choice,' Ms Stowe went on. 'You either grasp it, try, and yes – maybe fail. But try! Or you let them walk all over you.'

We sat in silence. The air hummed.

Ms Stowe stood up. 'Norah, warm up. You're going on.'

I'd never moved so fast. Unzipping my anorak, stretching and star jumping on the spot while the rest of the team stood up in a quiet magical silence, taut like racehorses.

The game was the hardest I'd ever played. The opposition were bigger and stronger than us, but when we got the ball we were nippier and more strategic. More determined. Like David and Goliath, weaving through and catching them off guard. Malaika scored a majestic goal from the very corner of the circle that made the remaining crowd gasp. Intrigued, people started drifting over to watch. Gradually the score crept up.

By the last quarter we were still down, but the opposition were suddenly within reach.

'All or nothing, girls,' said Ms Stowe as we panted next to her, sucking on our water bottles. 'Ten minutes left. Anyone can do anything in ten minutes. Yes!'

'Yes!' we said in unison. Fuelled and ready.

'You're my girls,' Ms Stowe said, and I wondered if I saw a tear of pride in her eye.

Then two minutes into play, Bettina got elbowed in the face and smashed down to the tarmac. The game was paused while a bleeding Bettina was led off court. Ms Stowe ordered Anouschka to take my bib, Malaika to take Bettina's and me to take Malaika's, which put me into goal shooter.

My eyes widened. 'I can't shoot.'

'Yes you can,' Ms Stowe replied. 'Just keep your focus.'

There was no time to quibble because the umpire's whistle blew.

Play was rougher and more frenetic. Goals were being scored left, right, and centre, although not by me. I made it my job to get the ball into the circle so Malaika could shoot.

The crowd grew. Chelsea High flags waved. Time was running out.

From the corner of my eye, I saw Laurent stroll over with Yannis and Emir. I felt a jolt at the sight of him, but looked away. This was what Ms Stowe meant by focus. In less than ten minutes I could look, I could feel, I could think. Right now, all that mattered was that ball.

The score was suddenly even. There was no more than a

minute left. I had the ball, but I couldn't find Malaika, who was blocked in by the defence.

'Just shoot, Norah!' Malaika shouted.

I tried to get the ball to her, but it was no good. Time was ticking. And I wondered suddenly if I *was* afraid of winning. If I *did* feel like I didn't deserve it.

It was much easier not to try.

'Just shoot,' Malaika called again.

I shot. I was tired of being afraid, of hiding in shadows. I wanted to fight. We deserved to win. I shot on instinct. No distraction. All my focus. The outside world a blur. Heart pumping. The crowd holding their breath.

I missed.

The ball rounded the metal rim of the net and missed.

The crowd sighed. At least I'd tried.

But as the ball bounced off the net, Malaika caught it. And just as the umpire put the final whistle to her lips, she scored the winning goal.

I had never been happier for anyone in my life.

CHAPTER THIRTY-ONE

The rest of the morning was a blur of happiness. The headmaster presented us with our medals, all shiny and gold. Ms Stowe was ecstatic. Bettina came back, face grinning, steri-stripped by the school nurse and on crutches for her twisted ankle. It was the first time we properly felt like a team.

We watched some of the other matches. Cheered on the girls' hockey. Layla wanted to watch the cricket, but I had no interest in watching Rollo so I went to see some of the gymnastics. Everything seemed brighter, the sky bluer.

Later on, I sat in a deckchair next to Malaika, medals round our necks. She reached over and squeezed my hand. I squeezed hers back.

'We did it,' she whispered.

I saw her grinning, and smiled. 'We did it.'

I felt bigger and braver and stronger, alongside a prickle of apprehension. I had let something into my life and I wasn't a hundred per cent sure how to control it. I had shown myself my own courage and I couldn't shy away now.

A trumpet fanfare cut through my thoughts. The boys' polo final was about to start.

'You watching?' Malaika asked.

'I don't know.' I shielded my eyes and looked over at the gathering crowd. It was enormous, ten times that of the netball. 'Are you?'

'I think so.' Malaika hauled herself out of the deckchair. 'Emir, Yannis and Laurent were cheering for us.' When she said Laurent's name, she looked at me for a reaction.

'I don't think Laurent actually cheered,' I said wryly.

We ambled over to the field where the boys were doing warm-up circuits. Laurent was out front, head bent, whispering to his pony, blind to the rest of the world. I'd never seen him so serious.

The umpire trotted out and blew a whistle.

The teams took their places. The air simmered. The crowd watched, excited. This was what they'd been waiting for.

Laurent's pony was so fired up it could barely stand still. I heard one of the mothers next to me say, 'That's him,' to her friend, who whistled under her breath. 'If only I was twenty years younger,' the friend murmured, and they both cackled quietly.

I realised Titus Summers was standing one away from my left, his hands clenched into white-knuckle fists by his side. He hadn't seen me, his attention focused purely on Laurent. I studied his profile. The line of his jaw. The hard-edged glint in his eye.

'What are you doing? Jesus!' he shouted, spittle flying,

making me jump. I realised play had started. 'For Christ's sake. Is the umpire even watching?'

The woman between him and me pursed her lips. 'Yannis isn't looking his best,' she muttered, lifting a tiny pair of mother-of-pearl binoculars to her eyes, giant diamonds on her fingers winking in the sun. Lavinia Summers. Caramel-blonde hair a shade lighter than Coco's, lean sinewy arms and sharp angular features. She looked like she had once been a model, and she smelt headily of Chanel No. 5.

'Yannis is never bloody looking his best,' Titus fumed. 'Shouldn't be on the team, if you ask me. I've told the coach numerous times.'

I felt myself bristle. I liked Yannis.

Laurent came thundering down the field, just behind a blue-shirted player from the other team, his pony's mouth frothy with spit, eyes blazing, charging at a speed that made me suck in my breath and made the crowd murmur. The other guy was fighting to stay ahead, but Laurent, in that state, was unbeatable.

I'd never seen him play before, and it made my breath catch.

The speed Laurent was going wasn't just madness. It was like diving head first into death. Spectators winced. But in a heartbeat Laurent had manoeuvred his pony, made the turn, taken control of the play and was already zigzagging back past players blocked by Emir and Freddie while the other guy was still trying to regain his composure.

Titus nodded, expressionless. 'Good play.'

Three chukkas down, I couldn't deny that Laurent was an incredible player. But that didn't mean he was a good sportsman. I didn't know that much about polo, but it looked like he played wild and dirty. Every time he did, his dad seemed to get a rush of pride. It was hard to watch someone look like they were out to kill themselves every time the whistle blew.

Last chukka, they all came out on new horses. Laurent was on sweet, lovely Mabel – his favourite pony.

Titus raised his hand and shouted, 'Give 'em hell, son!'

Laurent looked over with a sharp nod.

Then he saw me. I think it was the first time he'd even noticed the crowd.

I folded my arms across my chest, defensive, and saw the corner of his mouth tilt upwards. He sat up straighter, smugger. Mabel tossed her head.

Then he drew his brows together, staring across the field. Looked back at me, to see if I'd noticed.

I turned.

And I saw Ezra. Tall and imposing. Hair unruly. Beautiful, even from a distance. Our eyes locked just as the whistle blew for the final play.

'Get on with it!' Titus shouted. 'For Christ's sake, boy, what are you doing?!'

I tore my gaze from Ezra to see Laurent charging up the field, trying to catch up with the pack.

Ezra was here.

'Oh my god, is that Ezra?' Malaika said.

Ezra's mouth curved into a smile. He lifted his hand in a casual wave. I waved back, overwhelmed.

Play came back our way, Titus was still shouting. Hooves trembled the ground. Laurent was bearing down hard on the opposition, cutting dangerously close to one guy. The umpire blew his whistle. Titus swore. Laurent pulled back, eyes blazing.

I looked for Ezra again in the crowd, but he was gone. If Malaika hadn't noticed him, I'd have wondered if I'd imagined it. And then, suddenly there was a hand on my shoulder.

'Hey,' Ezra said softly.

'Hello,' I replied, uncertain.

We stood next to each other. The smell of him was so comforting. On instinct my body wanted to curl into him, but we didn't touch. Instead, we watched Laurent cutting and swerving, aggressive and powerful, heard Titus clap in delight.

I glanced up at Ezra, at the razor cut of his jaw, the messy curls, the crumpled T-shirt and black jeans. 'Why are you here?'

His dark eyes flashed. 'For you.'

The umpire's whistle blew again, drawing me back to the game. Titus hollered, 'You're blind!'

Laurent wasn't looking at the umpire. He was looking at us. At Ezra. He caught my eye for a fraction of a second, then pulled on the reins and tore the pony back up the field.

Titus was pumped. So was Laurent.

'Are you watching this?' Ezra asked, nodding towards the game, clearly wanting to move away.

I wanted to go, but found I couldn't leave. 'There's not that long left,' I said.

'No hurry,' Ezra said. He allowed his arm to drop, right close to mine so our skin was touching. Warm and familiar.

The scoreboard showed Chelsea High in the lead, but play was chaotic and the other team suddenly drew level.

'What are you doing?' Titus screamed at Laurent when he missed a shot. 'Concentrate, you idiot!'

Next to Titus, Lavinia said, 'It was a difficult cut shot.'

'It wasn't bloody difficult, he's not bloody concentrating, that's the problem. For Christ's sake, Laurent!'

I felt my body get hot. I wanted Titus Summers to be quiet. I knew we were a distraction, me and Ezra. But this was Laurent. He won at all costs. I told myself it wouldn't matter if I was there or not. I wanted to see the game play out. Or maybe I just wanted to see him play.

I didn't know if Laurent could hear his father or not. His face was stony. He shouted something at Yannis, who gave him a thumbs up and in turn made a gesture to Emir who nodded.

There couldn't be long left. Mabel was sweating, frothing at the mouth, agitated by the shouts of the crowd. I watched, transfixed, as Laurent leaned forward with a gentle touch of her neck and whispered something in her ear.

The game was too far away for me to see what was going on, but Lavinia was commentating from her binocular view.

'Yannis has it. Straight to Laurent. Nice blocking –'

'Let me see.' Titus grabbed the binoculars. 'Brilliant,' he breathed. 'Bloody brilliant, go on, my boy.'

Laurent was whizzing up the field, the opposition held back by Yannis, Freddie and Emir, leaving the path clear. Head down, eyes steely. Beneath him, Mabel flew. It was mesmerising.

Then suddenly, the blue-shirted guy from before shot out of nowhere, sneaking up the outside, trying to emulate Laurent's previous play.

'Has Laurent seen him?' Lavinia asked with obvious concern. It didn't look like it.

'What the bloody hell's this idiot doing? He's going to get himself killed. WHAT ARE YOU DOING?' Titus shouted.

'Watch out!' I shouted, my heart in my throat.

The other guy was cutting across, almost level, too close. Laurent suddenly saw him.

'Keep going!' Titus shouted.

They were too close. The guy was out of control. If Laurent carried on straight, they would collide.

'It's a bloody penalty! Where's the umpire?' Titus roared. 'Laurent, keep it up! He'd better not bloody waver!'

Please turn, I begged, silently. *Please turn.*

Closer and closer.

Laurent pressed on.

Mabel stumbled slightly but kept going. Eyes wild.

Laurent glanced up. His eyes locked tight with mine.

I couldn't breathe.

The other guy was way too close. His pony clipped Mabel and he lost control, toppling like he was about to fall.

'Go for it! Take it home!' Titus hollered.

But instead Laurent cut sharp to the left, abandoning play. Giving the guy space to regain control of his horse, to right himself, to save himself from being trampled underfoot by a dangerous muddle of tangled pony hooves. Saving Mabel.

In the process, I watched as if in slow motion, the swerve Laurent had to make, like a motorbike skidding rounding a corner. It threw him from Mabel's back, hard to the ground. There was a loud crack, like something in his body snapped.

I gasped.

Ezra winced.

The whistle blew.

No win for Chelsea High.

'Jesus Christ!' Titus was beside himself as Laurent lay flat on his back, motionless. The medic was running towards him, but Titus seemed oblivious to the injury, striding across the field towards his son. 'What the hell kind of move was that? You could have had him!'

Laurent lifted his hand to his face, covering his eyes, as

Titus stood over him, yelling, 'Get up!'

The medic was on his knees beside Laurent, trying to assess the injury while also keeping Titus at arm's length.

'I said, get up!' Titus shouted again.

Laurent blew out a breath of pain as he attempted to lift himself off the ground. The medic urged him not to move. Lavinia tottered over and tried to quell Titus's anger, but he was too far gone to rein himself in.

It was the medic who came between them, standing up and clearly and calmly telling Titus to leave. Which he did with a disgusted shake of his head, marching away across the field, leaving Laurent lying on his back staring up at the sky.

CHAPTER THIRTY-TWO

The crowd closed in around Laurent. Yannis, Freddie and Emir along with the coach and various grooms came to his aid, then a wave of friends from his year.

Ezra nudged my arm to beckon me away, someplace quieter where we could talk. We walked together to the old cracked bench outside the changing rooms. I had to fight the urge to check what was happening back on the field with Laurent.

Ezra's hand brushed mine as we walked. I glanced across at his profile, his dark hooded eyes and the sharp line of his nose. Familiarly handsome and dishevelled. Awkward and artful. His skin pale like he hadn't slept properly in weeks.

The hockey boys were using the bench to take off their boots. Their faces lit up when they saw Ezra, who'd coached them for a while. 'Did you see us?' they asked, crowding round, their hands finding reasons to touch him, to adore him.

I waited, leaning against the changing-room wall until Ezra could extract himself.

'Sorry,' he said with a smile, crooked and angular.

'That's all right,' I replied, trying not to be equally adoring, my body thrumming with realisation that he was here for me. 'You can't disappoint your fans.'

He stood alongside me, his shoulder propped up against the crumbling brickwork. 'You're the only one I don't want to disappoint.'

You already have. The reply was instant, silent, inside myself.

He reached across and touched my arm, slowly, like he wasn't sure if he was allowed. I felt the stroke of his fingers against my skin.

'I'm really sorry, Norah. I've never been more sorry for anything.' His big, forlorn eyes locked on mine. 'I was angry and I was a fool, basically. Mixed up. The only thing I regret more is that I hurt you as much as I hurt myself.' He half laughed. 'And it really bloody hurts.'

He was so close. So tall. His smell so familiar and inviting, his face so achingly attractive. My whole body drew towards him like the tide. I belonged with him. When he took a step forward, I didn't step away.

Then suddenly Coco's silken voice cut in. 'Ahhhh, isn't this sweet,' she said.

Verity was with her. So were Emmeline and Rollo, draped round each other as usual.

Coco was still in her polo kit, her hair tumbling glossy down her back. The girls had won their tournament, and Coco had scored most of the goals. I imagined she played as dirty as Laurent, but I was pretty sure her dad didn't care as much if she won. She was sucking on a strawberry lolly that had dyed her mouth dark crimson. Twisting it from between her lips, she held the lolly to one side and said, 'Is this a reunion? How touching.'

Ezra glanced heavenward. 'Hi, Coco.'

She gave a sly little grin. 'Hi, Ezra.'

I wanted him to tell her to go away. He didn't. Instead, we all stood there uncomfortably.

'Well.' Coco smiled, dangerously light and breezy. 'We don't want to interrupt you two lovebirds any longer. Come on.' She beckoned to Verity, Rollo and Emmeline. Then she paused as if she'd forgotten something. 'Oh, Norah, just in case you're worried, they think Laurent's broken his arm. It'll mess up his polo, but he's going to be fine.'

I kept my face impassive.

She licked her lolly. Said to Ezra, 'They're together, you know. Norah and my brother.'

Ezra stiffened. Verity bit her lip, delighted.

'Laurent and I are not together,' I said flatly.

Coco feigned surprise. 'That's not what I heard. I heard it's been *very* friendly between the two of you. Cosy evenings on your boat.'

I felt my cheeks get hot. 'You don't know what you're talking about!'

A voice came out of nowhere. A soft, confident drawl. 'Don't believe a word of it. We kissed once, and it was me that kissed her. It was entirely my fault.'

Laurent was standing, his face ashen, his arm strapped in a sling packed with cold compresses, flanked by Yannis, Emir and two paramedics in dark green, with his mum a few steps behind, struggling in her heels. The paramedic was trying to urge him on past us to the car park where an ambulance was waiting,

I found myself cutting in, wanting to own my responsibility in the events. 'It wasn't entirely his fault. I was just as much to blame –'

Looking Ezra straight in the eye, Laurent said, 'There's nothing between us, mate. Honestly. She hasn't done anything.'

I refused to hide from this any longer. 'But I *have* done something!' I said. Enough of the lies and the game play. 'Just what we did wasn't wrong.'

Laurent looked taken aback. He glanced warily at Ezra, then back to me, apologetic. 'I was just trying to help,' he said.

I bit my lip, consumed by a wave of emotion for him, broken and despondent but still trying to hold it together.

Laurent's face split into a pained grin. 'Take care of her, Ez. It's you she wants, not me. Don't mess it up again.'

Ezra gave a curt nod, tight-lipped and jaw rigid. Laurent nodded back, then winced suddenly with pain. The paramedics took over, urging him swiftly but carefully to the ambulance.

Coco smiled smugly. 'See?'

'Go somewhere that's not where we are, Coco,' I said with

quiet authority. I'd had enough of other people controlling my life.

Verity practically snarled as she started to speak in Coco's defence.

I shook my head. 'Not interested, Verity. Coco, your brother is being taken off in an ambulance and you're here trying to cause trouble in a relationship that you've already split up! Don't you see how messed up that is? My god, if you put as much energy into building relationships as you did in destroying them, you would have more than just Verity as your friend.'

'I have plenty of friends, thank you very much,' snapped Coco.

'Good,' I said. 'Go and hang out with them.'

I walked away, tapping Ezra on the arm as an indication he could come with me if he wanted. He did, leaving Coco to steam in her own fury.

We sat on the edge of the empty hockey pitch, where we had once sat before, when our relationship was teetering on the cusp of something. The caretaker was up a ladder, unhooking Chelsea High bunting. The air smelt of fresh cut grass and afternoon sun.

Ezra said, 'Did you kiss him?'

'Yeah.'

Ezra absorbed the information.

'But you and I weren't together at the time,' I said.

He ran a frustrated hand through his hair. 'I can't bear it,' he said. 'The idea of him with you. Don't trust him, Norah.'

Something inside me snapped. I thought of Emmeline, lost in Rollo. This wasn't about Ezra, or even about Laurent. It was about me. My decisions. My life.

'You can't tell me not to trust him,' I said.

'Sorry?'

I looked at his dark, muddled eyes. 'I said, you can't tell me not to trust him. I trusted you. And look where that got me.'

'Norah, I've said I'm sorry,' he urged, expression agonised and a little hard done by. 'What more can I say?'

'I know you have,' I agreed. 'And I accept your apology.'

I thought of how I had wanted to reach out and touch him, to lean my head against his arm and for him to kiss my hair and wrap his arm tight round me and for us to sit watching the bunting fall softly to the grass. A month ago his apology would have been enough. Back then, I was trying to live a fairy tale. Moulding myself to fit the part, in order to hold the world steady. But what about me? Where did I go in the process?

If I gave in to Ezra, then I was selling myself short. I wanted the fairy tale, but what I had was real life. I thought of what my mum had said the night before, about it being hard to make a big change in your life, how you could get scared.

Ezra was so hauntingly beautiful, so damaged, so close,

so mine. He cupped my face with his hands. 'Please, Norah. I need you.'

Our foreheads touched. My eyes welled with tears.

'I don't think you're in the right place for a relationship, Ezra. You have too much else to deal with right now.'

'That's not true,' he said, urging me to stop. 'I've learned from this. I've changed, believe me. Norah, I love you.'

I wanted more. I deserved more. It was so hard, but I shook my head.

'I'm sorry,' I said, voice wavering.

Ezra looked at me with disbelief. He had flown over to sort things out. How could this be happening? His head jerked up as if he'd suddenly nailed the problem.

'Is this because of Laurent?' he asked, eyes slightly accusing.

I shook my head, feeling suddenly clear-sighted and strong, like the grandmother I'd never met who claimed that true love did not conquer all. 'You're not ready, Ezra. You felt hemmed in by me, so you slept with Coco. What happens the next time I'm jealous? What happens with the next problem we face? You're under too much pressure already with your brother and your family. It's too much. I can't live afraid of what might happen. I love you, but this is not the right time for us.'

There was a pause.

Then Ezra said, voice tight, 'Laurent will hurt you more than I have.'

I couldn't help but laugh. 'It's not a competition.

I'm not going to let anyone hurt me, Ez.'

He nodded down at the grass. 'I'm sorry. I shouldn't have said that.'

I put my hand on his arm. Squeezing it gently, not wanting to let go. He put his hand on top of mine, looked me straight in the eye.

'This isn't the end, Norah,' he said, determined.

I didn't reply.

He shook his head, exhaled long and slow. 'I can't believe this.'

And as he looked at me with those sad brown eyes, it felt like I was cracking right down the centre. There it was, the pain I'd been waiting for. This was what heartbreak felt like.

CHAPTER THIRTY-THREE

As I walked through the empty school corridors, I could hear the piano warming up for the Variety Performance. Ezra had left. Maybe one day our time would come again. Or maybe not.

I paused at the double doors to the Great Hall. There was Daniel, glasses on, scurrying around with bits of paper and his clipboard. A row of tap dancers were on stage, trying to fine tune their choreography in the time they had before curtain-up.

A group of younger kids were being taken through their harmonies by Ms Venn, barely able to stand still with excitement, half dressed in their costumes already. I smiled when the little soloist piped up, her gold lamé tutu ruffling as she swayed to the song.

The air was humming with nerves.

I don't know how long I watched for. Enough time to get lost in the thrill of it all. The countdown, the nervous laughter, the fizz of anticipation, the ear-splitting loudness of the sound test, the flashing of the spotlights as the lighting crew tested the rig, the call to the stage for the warm-up. Just the sight of everyone in their leggings and vests, their baggy T-shirts and shorts, their half-done hair and partial make-up was enough to make me burn with envy.

'Do you miss it?' asked Mr Benson, our Theatre Studies teacher, appearing next to me, laden down with programmes as he too peered through the half-open doors.

I shrugged, trying and failing to appear blasé. 'A bit.'

He pushed his glasses up his nose with his shoulder, dropping some of the programmes as he did. I bent and picked them up for him.

'Thank you,' he said as I added them as best I could to the pile in his arms. 'I do too.'

He perched on one of the green chairs that visitors sat in when waiting to go into the headmaster's office across the corridor. 'I just used to adore being on the stage. There's nothing else quite like it. I was never the lead in anything. My mother would say "I shone from the sidelines", which of course was an absolute lie, but I liked it.'

I smiled at the idea of a young Mr Benson.

'I know you haven't wanted to have anything to do with the show,' he continued, 'but now the netball is over, I wondered if maybe . . .' He struggled to phrase his question. 'Well, you see, Portia Cox has shingles and won't be able to perform. She didn't have a big role, but it does rather throw out the symmetry and, well, I don't know if you'd be happy to just be in the chorus?' He gave a nervous laugh as the band started up, loud and engulfing. 'As my mother said, you too could "shine from the sidelines". If you wanted that is. No pressure –'

'Yes!' I cut off his rambling before I had time to think about it. There was nothing in that moment I wanted more. 'Yes,' I repeated. 'I'll be in the chorus.'

Mr Benson looked taken aback that I'd agreed so readily. 'Marvellous. I'll tell Daniel. He'll run through the moves with you. It'll be quite an intensive hour or so, if that's OK?'

'That's absolutely fine,' I said.

There could be nothing better right now than being lost in music.

And it was glorious. Everything I wanted it to be. Like the netball but simply more me. Like singing with my mum, I could feel the magic seep back into me. It helped that I was in costume, dressed the same as everyone else in hot-pink satin shorts and a white frilly top with giant feathers in my hair, my face embellished and almost unrecognisable under all the make-up and glitter. It was all flooding back, loud and intoxicating, and I let it in in all its glorious, nerve-wracking, adrenaline-fuelled Technicolor.

Coco strutted about backstage in a cream silk dress and glitter-sprayed hair. Freddie was in a tux, roguishly cool with the top button undone and his hair all askew. They brought the house down with their song and dance number, got a roaring standing ovation. I watched, a little bit jealous. But

I was beginning to realise that even envy was better than feeling nothing.

Every now and then, I wondered how Laurent was, if he was thinking about me. Did he wonder what had happened with Ezra? Or had he moved on to the next thing already?

I left the Variety Performance on a high. Daniel had recorded me in it on my phone, so I could show my dad the next day at visiting – give him something to smile about.

I cycled home in a good mood, swerving for traffic, humming the tunes. My lips were still painted shocking pink, my hair still plaited around the side of my head and threaded with ribbon, my glitter-rimmed eyes more open than ever to the world around me.

I think that was why the police car stood out so brightly. A stark white against the blackness of the river.

I pulled up slowly at the entrance of the jetty, craning my neck to see our boat. The lights were on. I approached slowly, wheeling my bike to the railing of our deck. I could hear voices inside. How stupid I had been to let my guard down, to think this part of things was somehow over.

Standing in the kitchen of our boat were DC Burnley and DS Martin, looking exactly as they had on Mulberry Island – him in his black bomber jacket, her with her long beige mac and beady magpie eyes.

'What's happened?' I asked, wishing I wasn't covered in glitter.

There was a panama hat hanging on the peg. I looked round to see my grandparents and Harold their butler. My grandmother, all tanned and wearing new summer clothes, had a woollen shawl over her shoulders and was tucked into the corner of the sofa with a cup of tea. My granddad was standing by the window, a large brandy in his hand. Mum stood by the counter.

'There's been a robbery,' said Mum, eyes piercing into mine.

All I could think about was the dog. 'Is Ludo OK?' I asked, imagining him shot and mortally wounded.

'Yes bloody Ludo's OK,' said my granddad, perplexed by the question. 'Fattening up in kennels, living the life of Riley, which is more than can be said for us. Bastards invading my house. How dare they?'

'I can't go back there,' said my grandmother, fists screwed in anger. 'The idea of them rifling through my things. It's horrific.'

'What did they take?' I asked, aware of DS Martin's eyes on me.

'Whatever they could get their hands on,' said my grandmother. 'Watches, jewellery, TV, all the good art. Do you know, they even took my Louboutins?'

'I told you not to buy such expensive shoes,' huffed my granddad. 'Somehow or other they got into the damn safe.'

'They can do anything nowadays,' said my grandmother.

'Anyone want tea?' said Mum, not looking at me.

Had my dad repaid the favour by giving Vincent the code

to the safe and details of all the good stuff in his own parents' house? Was he one of them now? Part of the Spider's Web?

'There's more, Norah.' This time it was DC Burnley's turn to speak. 'We had a call. An anonymous tip-off with a date and time for the burglary, which meant our officers were waiting.'

My granddad was nodding, impressed. 'Caught two of the little creeps. Very efficient. That's British policing for you. You can always rely on Scotland Yard.'

DC Burnley nodded, proudly accepting the compliment.

'Although catching all three would have been better,' my granddad added. 'Then I'd still have two of my Picassos.' DC Burnley pinked a touch.

'Who was the tip-off from?' I asked.

'It was *anonymous*,' said DS Martin, repeating the word like I hadn't understood. I could imagine her internally mocking my childish stage make-up. 'The call was made on a burner phone somewhere in the central London area. Any ideas, Norah?'

I immediately thought of my dad and the mobile phone he'd borrowed before. Had he purposely double-crossed Vincent? Did he think by doing so, he was protecting his parents? That was his kind of logic. But surely if he'd made the call in jail, they'd have traced the location. God. Had he asked someone else? Did he owe another favour? I prayed he knew what he was doing.

My grandmother was looking confused. 'How the devil would Norah have any idea?'

DS Martin shrugged. 'Kids nowadays know everything, don't they?'

My grandmother harrumphed. The atmosphere frosted over with silence.

'Custard cream, anyone?' said Mum.

DC Burnley said, 'Don't mind if I do.' And took two.

I remembered offering Vincent biscuits from the same packet and wondered how DC Burnley would feel about that.

'What happens now?' Granddad asked rather briskly, putting his empty brandy glass on the kitchen counter a touch too hard.

DC Burley cleared his throat. 'The SOCO team should be done by now, so you can go back to the house, sir. I'd suggest changing the locks. The valuables we have recovered will be kept as evidence for the time being. Anything else of value, we would recommend moving from the property.'

'What a pain,' Granddad grumbled. 'And the next steps? Identifying the suspects? Witnesses? Court?'

'We'll be in touch, sir,' said DC Burnley.

The officers headed to the door. DS Martin suddenly looked straight at me.

'If anyone has anything they think might be relevant to the case,' she said, 'do get in touch.'

Mum came to stand beside me, both of us conscious that

we were withholding information. Our world was merging with my dad's as we chose loyalty over justice. It wasn't right, but it was love.

CHAPTER THIRTY-FOUR

When the phone rings in the middle of the night, it's never good. I fumbled awake, bleary-eyed and confused.

'Oh my god. Is he going to be OK?' Mum was saying. 'How has this happened? You're meant to keep him safe!'

We sat silently in the taxi on the way to the hospital, Mum's hand holding tight to mine. It was four in the morning. I had thrown tracksuit bottoms on over my star pyjamas and a long cardigan of Mum's. I was shivering.

At two-thirty that morning, the door to my dad's cell had been unlocked. He had been dragged out of bed by his ankles and suffered what was considered to be systematic and premeditated injuries. Which meant they did just enough not to kill him. They knew what they were doing.

The door was locked again from the outside.

His room-mate alerted the guards, having apparently slept through the whole attack.

No one would tell us anything more. We didn't know the extent of his injuries. We sat in the hospital waiting area, waiting for the sun to rise, and visiting times to begin.

My mum begged the prison guard to let us see him, but he shook his head, emotionless.

I slept a little with my head on my mum's shoulder, hours ticking by in the fluorescent lights and organised chaos of A&E. My grandparents arrived in a bluster of questions and allegations. They berated the prison guard. They called their lawyer.

I sat and watched the door behind which my dad was lying in a bed, machines monitoring the beat of his heart.

When they finally let us in the room – 'Five minutes,' said the guard, eye on the clock – Dad could only open one puffy eye. He was barely recognisable: nose broken, one side of his face the multicolours of a bruise, his leg in plaster, his arm in a sling, his ribs bandaged. His body was a patchwork of cuts and bruises. When he tried to smile, half his teeth were missing. He sucked on a glass of water through a straw.

My mum broke down on the faux-leather visitors' chair.

'I'm OK,' Dad murmured. 'Or at least, I'm not dead.' He winced with pain as he tried to laugh.

'It's not funny, Bill!' said Mum. 'You could have been killed.'

'I was just unlucky,' mumbled my dad.

'Don't give me that. I know everything, Bill. Norah told me.'

'This isn't the time for secrets, Dad,' I said softly.

He nodded, accepting this. Then he was back asleep again. My mum held his hand for the few minutes we had left, and I stood next to her, staring at his battered face.

I wondered if Vincent thought the favour had been repaid.

By Sunday afternoon, my dad was sitting up in bed. There was a different guard on the door and he was laughing at something my dad had said, bantering. When we arrived, he didn't issue the strict visiting time limit, although he made my mum leave the grapes and satsumas she'd brought outside the door.

We sat round the bed, my mum fussing, smoothing down the sheets, plumping the pillows. 'You look much better,' she said.

'I don't know about that,' said Dad, wincing.

I held his hand, cool and rough and familiar. There were grazes across his knuckles, maybe from where he defended himself, maybe from where he fell.

'Why didn't they kill you?' I asked quietly.

My mum stopped straightening the sheets. My dad peered round to see that the officer was too busy flirting with the desk nurse to overhear.

'Because the police didn't catch them all,' he replied. 'People talk while they're kicking the shit out of you.' He tried for a laugh, but it was clearly too painful. 'They let me know that Vincent was satsified with the Picassos. That's god knows how many millions for him. He's nothing but fair.'

So everyone had come away with something. Vincent had

got some Picassos, the police had got some criminals. It wasn't great for my grandparents, but at least they hadn't been home, and they were insured, and no one was hurt, not even the dog.

'But that wasn't what you thought would happen,' I whispered. 'It was luck that one guy got away.'

My dad grinned. 'Life is luck, Norah. What else have we got?' He shuffled himself up the bed, looking a bit sheepish. 'I suppose I was hoping Vincent wouldn't know it was me that tipped off the police.'

My mum rolled her eyes. 'For goodness' sake, who else would they think it was?'

'But it wasn't you,' I said. 'You couldn't have called from jail.'

The police officer stuck his head in the door to check that we weren't up to no good.

'All above board in here, officer,' my dad joked with a smile that looked like agony.

The policeman chuckled and disappeared again. After a pause Dad said, 'Did you know Tricky asked to be put on my visitor list? Nice to see a friendly face from the island.'

'Did he?' my mum said, surprised. 'We saw him the other day too, what a coinciden—'

She stopped. We all exchanged glances. My dad nodded.

I lowered my voice. 'But why would Tricky put himself at such risk?'

'Why would he be part of such a stupid plan, more like?'

my mum muttered.

My dad shrugged. 'Because he's a good friend.'

Perhaps Tricky had done it because he knew otherwise my dad might have to rely on someone else inside. Or perhaps he had done it so we didn't have to. To make sure we stayed innocent, on our side of the world. Or maybe my dad was right, it was purely out of friendship. It fuelled my memory of the island as a family, as a place where people stuck together whatever happened. Something I had feared was lost.

My dad coughed and his face contorted in agony.

Mum stood up. 'I'm going to find the nurse and get you more painkillers.'

Alone in the room together, my dad looked down at his arm in the sling, the hospital sheets, the gown, and said, as if he couldn't bring himself to look at me, 'I think I just wanted to save the day.'

He looked suddenly so small and vulnerable. My heart tugged.

'I was so worried when you rang,' Dad said. 'I didn't want Vincent on the boat or anywhere near you. I wanted him to come after me instead. I didn't care much what happened to me.'

I looked at him, frail and beaten but somehow recharged. His schemes would always be hare-brained, but this was the first time I'd heard about a scheme that hadn't been for himself. It had been for me. And for Mum. Because those relationships were worth it. And in one fell swoop, that sacrifice made up for all the disappointments in the past.

'I care,' I said, squeezing tight on his hand. 'I care what happens to you.'

Something passed between us. His eyes were large and watery with relief, like I was offering him something he had thought was lost. Forgiveness. Maybe love.

And I was.

I was no longer ashamed. I was no longer angry. I just knew he was my dad. And while his heroism had been ridiculous, I was proud of him all the same. It felt like a new beginning.

I hugged him as gently as I could. 'I love you,' I whispered.

And he squeezed me back as hard as his broken ribs would allow.

My mum pushed the door open with a frustrated sigh. 'Why are there no nurses when you want one?'

I let go of my dad and beckoned my mum over to the corner of the room, just out of Dad's earshot.

'You have to tell him about the DNA test, Mum,' I said, trying my best to keep my nervous voice from wavering. 'You have to tell him so there aren't any secrets.'

Her face visibly fell. 'No!'

'You have to,' I said, steeling myself. 'Or I will.'

Because I knew there was nothing worse than being kept in the dark. The secret wasn't just between me and Mum now. Titus knew, and Laurent and Coco. And they could have no more hold on our family. There could be no more lies. No more false promises. It was hard enough keeping our two worlds aligned as it was. Secrets and lies didn't disappear if you ignored them. They took root and spread.

My mum's mouth opened in shock. 'Norah –'

I held her gaze. 'It's for the best.'

I hoped she understood. I looked back at my dad. He was toying with the knot at the back of his sling, oblivious.

Mum walked to Dad's bed without looking at me, straight-backed, face set.

'Bill,' she said, perching on the chair by his bedside. 'I have to tell you something.'

CHAPTER THIRTY-FIVE

Would my dad forgive her? Yes. He adored her. Worshipped her. Needed her. It would change them, and it would change us. But that was the thing about change. You could grip on tight, trying to hold it back, but it would drag you behind it anyway. The trick was getting ahead of the wave, learning to ride it, eyes open, into the unknown.

The sun was blinding through the revolving door of the hospital. I could see the sky, big and bright and beckoning. Out the front, buses arched to a hissing stop, ambulances wailed past and black taxis U-turned on a dime.

I stepped out into the sunshine, past a guy on a drip finishing a cigarette and a woman crying into a mobile phone. Beside me, pigeons fought over half a sandwich. I stood for a moment on the pavement, the sun glinting on car windscreens and warming the concrete beneath my feet.

'Norah?'

To my surprise, Laurent was strolling out of the hospital just behind me, arm in a sling, stitches on a cut along his cheekbone. He had a white T-shirt on, stretched out of shape around the neck, like he'd had trouble getting it on with his injuries, and khaki board shorts. His hair was a mess. He looked really tired. But he was still smiling, like always, eyes creasing at the sides.

I felt that familiar tingle of excitement at the sight of him.

'What are you doing here?' he asked. 'Did you come to visit me?' he added with dry mischief.

I shook my head. 'My dad's here.' I thought about how strongly I had kept those worlds apart. Pressed the lid down with shame. 'He got beaten up in jail.'

'No way,' said Laurent. 'Is he all right?'

'I hope so.' I gestured to Laurent's injuries. 'How about you?'

He shrugged, eyes twinkling. 'I'll be OK.'

I suddenly found that I didn't quite know how to talk to him. I wanted to say well done in the polo, for pulling back, for going against his dad. But I couldn't say anything, blocked by a sudden self-conscious shyness.

We stood together on the hospital forecourt. The pigeons were still fighting over the sandwich.

Laurent said, 'How'd things go with Ezra?'

'We broke up,' I replied.

There was a pause. I could feel his eyes on me. I tried to stop myself, but I looked back at him. I couldn't help it.

He was smiling. 'That's too bad,' he said.

A familiar dark green Range Rover pulled up at the curb. The window wound down and Wilson, Laurent's chauffeur, leaned over from the driver's seat.

'Morning,' he said with a tip of his head in recognition to me. 'All set, Laurent?'

Laurent nodded. 'Yeah, all fine.' Then to me, he said, 'Do you need a lift home?'

'No thanks,' I said, sad suddenly that he was leaving. 'I'm going to walk.'

He started towards the car. I stayed where I was. He was just opening the door when he turned back my way.

'How about I walk with you?' he asked. 'If you don't mind. It's a nice day and . . .' He stopped. It was the first time I'd heard Laurent lost for words.

I tried to sound casual but I could hear the roar of my heart in my ears. 'I don't mind.'

He nodded. 'Good. OK then.'

I could see Wilson trying to suppress a smile.

'OK,' I said.

'OK,' Laurent repeated. His face spread into the widest grin. 'See you later, Wilson.'

'Very good.'

Laurent held out his good arm for me to hook mine through, like we were some promenading Victorian couple. I hesitated. He nodded encouragingly, eyes alight.

I listened for my instinct. For what felt right. And I found myself slipping my arm through his as we walked, one foot in front of the other.

Was this the start of something? I had no idea. For now, we were just walking, secretly hoping it would take forever to get there.

ACKNOWLEDGEMENTS

A huge thank you to Sarah Levison and Lindsey Heaven for their intuitive and expert editorial insight and their enthusiasm for Norah and Chelsea High. Thanks also to Lucy Courtenay for her sharp-eyed refining skills, the fabulous Art, Production, Sales & Marketing and PR teams at Farshore Books, and my brilliant agent Rebecca Ritchie. It's been a tough year and everyone has worked above and beyond under uncertain and constantly changing circumstances. Thank you.

As a writer, you take things that have happened to you or situations you are familiar with and ramp them up to their highest level of conflict and excitement. I went to a school not dissimilar to Chelsea High – but without the added layer of gloss. It was cliquey and loud, bitchy and fun. You were friends one minute and arch enemies the next. You had to know yourself and find where you belonged, and that isn't easy as a teenager. I'd like to thank the whole rowing team for keeping me sane, for training in the only spot where they'd let us do free weights – the old, smelly changing rooms – and the coach who made us do circuits rather than audition when the modelling agency arrived at school, saving much humiliation!

I'd also like to thank Eel Pie Island (if you can thank an island!). I grew up round the corner from this quirky artists' community on the Thames – most famous for its hotel where bands like The Rolling Stones used to play. Walking among the bungalows and houseboats – buildings with giant ice-cream cones stuck to the roof and fake sharks in the garden – the idea of Norah and her eclectic family came into being. If you want to visit Eel Pie Island it's twenty minutes on the train from London Waterloo to Twickenham then you can either walk or take a five-minute bus journey to the island. If you want to see more of the inspiration behind Forever Summer then head to JennyOliverBks on Pinterest.

THE PATH OF TRUE LOVE NEVER RUNS SMOOTH

ENTER THE EXCLUSIVE WORLD OF...

Chelsea
HIGH

JENNY OLIVER